THE CALL

OF THE

ALLAGASH WILDERNESS

Canoeing the Allagash and other stories

The Call of the Allagash Wilderness

Published by Piscataqua Press
32 Daniel St., Portsmouth NH 03801
www.ppressbooks.com

Printed in the United States

ISBN: 978-1-950381-40-1

THE CALL

OF THE

ALLAGASH WILDERNESS

Canoeing the Allagash and other stories

Alexander H. ter Weele

Also by

Alexander H. ter Weele

We Escaped: A Family's Flight from Holland during World War Two
Piscataqua Press, 2015

Poems from the Blue Ridge
Piscataqua Press, 2017

Sir Alex Talks Soccer
Piscataqua Press, 2022

For

My Wife

Francine

FOREWORD

The stories in this collection were selected from works written over the course of my life. One dates back to the early 1960s; another was written in 2018. Some—for example, “The Maharajah and the Devil”—are obviously fictional. Others, such as “The Search for Solitude: Canoeing the Allagash,” describe personal experience; and yet others stem from observing a story unfold before my eyes, such as “The Psych Major,” which relates events experienced by a passenger I chatted with on a bus trip from Boston to New Orleans in 1963. “Two Worlds” recounts an incident when I was on board a mail boat delivering letters and packages to landlocked villages along the Turkish coast. The selection of stories is eclectic, and the variety is meant to ensure every reader finds at least one story he or she can enjoy. And given my many not-so-PC views, I am certain there will be at least one (or two or three) that will make some readers cringe with discomfort. But remember, discomfort can be a catalyst for thought, for analysis, and it can even lead to amused disagreement (rather than anger!) with an outrageous point of view.

Given the moment, I cannot but help dedicate this book

to my grandchildren. Seven years ago, one of them, as a first-grade assignment at Thanksgiving ("What are you thankful for?") wrote, "I am thankful for Opa. He can fix about anything in our house. He helped me with my 'Gadget Project.' Opa reads poems and books to me in the most wonderful way ever. Opa is the best grandfather in the world." And then, just days ago, as I was about to type this foreword, that same grandchild showed me her just-finished eighth-grade Hero Project ("Select a 'hero,' write a two-page essay about him/her, give a one-minute speech in the auditorium in front of 150 parents summarizing the essay.") The essay began "Who would imagine my hero would be the person who gave me my first spanking?!" And continued with (more pleasant but perhaps less vivid) memories, such as, "My grandfather and I every night sat by the fireplace reading *Curious George* and beautifully illustrated princess books. Then Opa would carry me on his shoulders and tuck me into bed with a song." And, "My family was going through a difficult time. My grandparents took us in with love and supported us. It could have been hard, but it wasn't." She concluded the essay with "I am told the first word I uttered was 'Opa,' so to love him was destiny!" Two days ago, in front of that audience of 150 persons, she concluded her speech by asking me to stand and, looking at me, said, "Although you don't hold my hand anymore, Opa, you will always hold my heart."

How, with all that, can I not dedicate this book to her? And, equally, how can I not include in the dedication the other dozen grandchildren as well? Each one has provided me scads of love and myriad moments that warmed my heart. In their order of birth: Alex, Simonne, Daniela,

Maria, Jakob, Jan, Joshua, Kiki, Nicolas, Lauren, Stafford, Everest, and (last but not least!) Margot. I love them all!

Alexander H. ter Weele
Caracole
December 2018

TABLE OF CONTENTS

THE SEARCH FOR SOLITUDE: CANOEING THE ALLAGASH

Is a retreat into the wilderness a search for solitude, for solace of the soul, or is it a romantic's wish to travel back in time to the Eden that was known to only a few people who lived in harmony with unspoiled nature? Or is it a search for the afterlife, a subconscious death wish, a desire to explore the happy hunting grounds before the hereafter arrives? As if, were the inevitable hereafter found unacceptable, one could arrest time's hands and refuse the ticket for the journey?

14 May 1998

I felt the pull yesterday morning as I left Bangor. First, the long sweep at high speed on Interstate 95 north. Space opening up. Wilderness beckoning. The industrial age, the technological age, the service economy slipping away. Fewer signs of man, and many of those agricultural and increasingly subsistence in nature. Broken, of course, by rude awakenings, eruptions of progress in the form of an industrial site or an intrusive conglomeration of mobile homes.

At Sherman, I abandoned the interstate and continued due north on Route 11. This road I drove some forty years ago in a mad midnight dash from Center Ossipee, New Hampshire, to Presque Isle, Maine. My brother was on Christmas leave from Loring Air Force Base. A panicked phone call screamed at him to return to base. Immediately. His leave had been cancelled. We ran for the car and dashed three hundred fifty miles north, where he sprinted for a 5 a.m. reveille and I turned the car on its heel for the six-hour drive back. All on Route 11. Hours and hours of Route 11. How did I drive twelve consecutive hours, up and back, all at night? My memory of it is so. Moonlight on snow. Moonlight on hemlock bogs frozen and white. Moonlight on vast potato fields. All white. All moonlight. All cold. All silent. Nothing. On the return trip, through one stretch of that northern bog with its moss, its pools of water, its humps, and its stunted hemlocks, I glanced at the odometer. For thirty-two miles, nothing. No house or light. No crossroad. No driveway or logging road. No pull-off. Nothing. Step off the tarmac and one would be knee deep in bog, entangled by brush.

Route 11 had changed since that madcap ride forty years ago, but the past was still there. The absolute wilderness, however, was no longer absolute. Man—or is it civilization? progress?—had left his mark, both in improvements and, alas and all too frequently, in excrement. Yet Boston, Portland, Bangor still had slipped away. Wilderness still encroached, enveloped. And increasingly, as I drove north up Route 11, I heard the call of the wild. A murmur at first, which would swell and ebb like a tide. When I arrived at Allagash, it was a delightful symphony. The Allagash spilling into the mighty St. John invoked music of Indian canoes as natives traded with early French settlers. The music of salmon running up to spawn, of grouse thrumming their welcoming rites to the coming spring, of moose bellowing into the night, of loons conversing with Indian spirits.

One image of this day's drive up Route 11 burned bright in my eye. Fields yellow with dandelions. At first, I thought it must be a planted crop. Rape seed, perhaps. But soon I could not deny that these were dandelions. Dandelions everywhere. The fields of sunflowers in Auvergne in early August are no more yellow than this. These pastures … Did they have any grass? Could cows graze them? It seemed there could be only dandelion plants, given the unblemished carpet of yellow. Gorgeous.

The town of Allagash pleased me. A few cabins along the road announced its coming. A bridge crossing the river, a river perhaps a hundred yards wide here, pinpoints the spot on the map where the Allagash spills into the St. John. Farther along, a few more houses, then a diner. Call this Allagash Village. To the north, the St. John River flows west to east, chopping the land into Canada to the north and the United States to the south. And the Allagash River reaching south into one of the largest remaining wilderness areas in the States.

I turned onto a gravel road running along the Allagash, followed it upstream for a short while. Southward. The river from Allagash Village to right here is tranquil, having vented its anger upstream. A modest current, enough to drive a canoe and to make paddling easy, but no great speed to the water. No rapids. No roils. No whitewater. A river that in England would be used by punters, a beau and his belle, on a Sunday afternoon. A river idolized by the Indians. A river that could be paddled upstream as well as downstream. A river providing access to the bounties of the wilderness, to hunting and fishing grounds, to myriad lakes to the south. A river that joined with the St. John to the north, and via the St. John to a further network of hundreds of streams and lakes, and the ocean as well.

At Allagash, I inquired and made acquaintance with Sean Lizotte, a professional guide. A young man, thirty perhaps, with a wife and two young children, a girl of five or six, a boy of three. He a touch above average height, cropped blond hair, lithe with the smooth movements of the creatures he hunts. For $130, he drove me, my canoe, and my gear up the network of gravel roads. We left his cabin and two dogs at 4:30 p.m. and arrived at the Thoroughfare, a bridge over the Allagash, where Umsaskis and Long Lake merge. His kids chattered the whole way. He shared his knowledge of these woods with me. We crossed paths with a she-bear and her cub, a pair of moose, a solitary moose, and then another pair of moose.

He dropped me in front of the ranger's cabin on the west side of the Thoroughfare, upstream from the bridge, on Umsaskis Lake. The ranger's boat and motor were there, but the ranger was nowhere to be seen. I pushed off in my canoe after I waved good-bye to Sean, who headed home to get his kids to bed. Camping is restricted to designated areas on the Allagash Waterway. The first campsite, in view of the bridge, I rejected. Too close to civilization. I had, after all, come in search of solitude. Ten minutes later, that search was rudely interrupted. Listening for the sounds of solitude, I heard instead the low vibration of a trolling motor. Around the point ahead of me came a johnboat with three fishermen. We exchanged hellos; I asked if they'd had any hits. They'd arrived at noon. Set up camp. Fished. Had dinner. Were fishing again. A whitefish or two. No trout.

Half an hour later, I came to the second campsite. It was invaded by their gear. An enormous tent. Another large tent. A tarp strung as a rain roof. Rucksacks. Cooking utensils. Plastic garbage bags. Although it was now late and the sun well into the trees, I paddled by. No solitude here. The next camping spot, marked on the map as *Sam's*, was free. No one there. From the signs, no one since last fall. I carried my gear behind the trees, and then shouldered my canoe behind them too. From the water, the site would appear unused. Important that, when searching for solitude. To see no one and to not be seen. The canoe canted to serve as a shelter, a quick can of beef stew, and to bed. It was getting too dark to see. And the night cold rushed around as the darkness settled.

At 4 a.m., it was light. Thank heavens for modern sleeping bags. The temperature had hovered at the freezing mark all night. In the bag it had been bearable, although I had the usual sore bones, the uncomfortable confinement of the bag, and the limited space under the canoe. I was startled into wakefulness by two moose that chanced upon me, then turned and fled. The snort and bang of hooves a canoe length from my sleeping bag shook me from my slumber. I tarried and then slid out of my covers.

Fog lay heavily on the lake. I added layers of clothes against the cold. My flannel shirt, which had lain on my face while sleeping to hide me from the frost, I wrapped around my neck like a scarf. The loons no longer called, but two woodpeckers drummed alternately on distant trees. First one, then a pause, and the second one would respond. After some minutes, a third bird joined the conversation. The sound carried distinctly in the mist. The sun rose, appearing over the hill. It glowed red momentarily and then disappeared as it rose into the bank of mist. I estimated it would reappear above the mist in an hour or so. Warm coffee and toast helped, but still I dallied. It was too cold to take action. Finally, I thawed out, packed the canoe, and slid soundlessly into the mist. The low thrumming of grouse sounded. Two ducks called each other. Farther along the shore, the music of spring water spilled into the lake. I searched and found it. Filled my bottles. As I pushed off a second time, the mist had lifted, and the lake and shore materialized.

I pulled onto the next point—a bar of gravel and sand, the sweep of the lake visible in both directions. Sign of two moose. Those that had awakened me? Older prints of a canine. A coyote, it would seem. And then an area with tufts of scattered fur. The coyote had caught a hare.

The sun warmed the world. I changed into my day clothes. Poked around the point, inspecting sights and sounds. Two loons appeared, nodded in greeting. I updated my diary as I sat in the sun. With a two-mile sweep of the lake in either direction, I sat for an hour. And another hour. Nothing. No one. No boats. No sign of man. Utter bliss. The call of a loon off the eastern shore. Heaven on earth. Solitude.

15 May 1998

The search continued, but this time in vain. After yesterday's midmorning entry in my diary, I canoed to Chemquasabamticook Stream on the west shore of Long Lake. I fished and canoed a mile or more upstream, through a winding delta of marsh grass and alder. Caught a trout, a brookie, on a green ghost. Eight inches of energy. Fully alive. The essence of Darwin's struggle of survival of the fittest. The epitome of the well adapted. At the other end of the "struggle" spectrum stands the moose that ambled out of the water a few minutes later. He also is well adapted, but his adaptation is one of predominance. So large, he has no true enemy. Except, of course, man. Because he has no true enemy and no need for fear, he also has no survival instinct. When man with a gun came on the scene, the moose was hunted out in a matter of decades. An easy quarry. No more difficult to stalk and shoot than a dairy cow grazing in a pasture. Only in the last quarter century, with strict protection, has the moose come back in numbers. Taller than any other forest browser, he eats buds and twigs that others cannot reach. He will "walk up" a small poplar or alder, bending it under his chest as he browses, reaching twigs that might, when not bent, hang ten feet in the air. His long forelegs help in this regard, as does his bulk. And those long legs and his enjoyment of water allow him to feed on aquatic plants well out from shore. The same long legs are his saviors in snow whose depth is the scourge of deer. Yes, the dominance of the moose was so complete that man's entry onto the scene precipitated his immediate decline. The trout, on the other hand, survives exactly because he is hunted. He has had to adapt to the struggle.

After Chemquasabamticook Stream, I returned to Long Lake, elated by its vista of open water and low hills. No touch of man. Vistas little altered over centuries except by the seasons and geologic evolution. Calm. Quiet. Space, empty space.

As I slid in the narrows between Long Lake and Harvey Pond, an alien sound intruded. To another it might have been an almost imperceptible drone. To me, a firecracker string of explosions. A few minutes later, a motorized canoe came upstream. The waterway ranger from Umsaskis Lake. He inquired where I had camped last evening and where I intended to camp tonight. He was cleaning up sites for the coming summer season. At any other time and place, his contact would be welcome, his knowledge and lore interesting and instructive. On a search for solitude, the contact was an intrusion.

Was it that brief encounter that transformed the Allagash from open water, long vistas, sun, and quietude into rushing rapids, narrow runs, darkness, and the roar of falling water? The next miles I traveled seemed somber, the rocks dangerous, the banks too near and forbidding. Care was required to avoid calamity. Just beyond Cunliffe Island, three moose grazed placidly in a backwater of open water. The sun and space reappeared. I paddled motionlessly upwind, a mere twisting of the paddle below the surface of the water, to within a few feet of them. I could have cast a fly onto their backs. A moose hooked on a green ghost at the end of a 4.4-pound tippet, thrashing about in knee-deep water, might not, I decided, be a good idea. I did not cast the fly. Moose are ugly this time of year. Gaunt. Patches of hair falling off their hides. Racks discarded, perhaps a few inches of replacement starting to grow. We watched each other warily for ten or fifteen minutes. Then I glided away, leaving them in their tranquility. The lion reigns as king of the jungle. The moose presides as country squire of the north woods.

At the end of Harvey Pond, a rush of water announced the remainders of Long Lake Dam. A sign instructed that "All Parties Portage." While one could probably run the rush of water between sunken beams and rocks, the spikes in the logs left from the dam recommended obeisance to the instruction. These remnants of industrial man's incursions into these distant north woods are reminders that modern man, despite what our ethnocentric egos would have us believe, is not a breed superior to those who went before. Upstream on this Allagash, on the shore of Eagle Lake, rusting locomotives squat curiously amidst trees, along the abandoned railway connecting Eagle with Umbazooksus Lake. And the bones of the tramway trace a straight line through the wilderness between Eagle and Chamberlain Lake. Hundreds of thousands of board feet of logs traveled these routes in the first part of the twentieth century. (The tramway was constructed in 1902–1903, the rail line in 1925–1926.) We are not superior, you see, than those who lived here a century ago. And we are not superior, either, to the Indians who subsisted here a millennium ago, even ten thousand years ago. Their tools were different. They were limited by their inability to store knowledge. Their lack of books, of written memory, required each generation to start afresh, except for what they could learn from their still-living elders. How long would we survive if dropped in these woods and forbidden contact with the outside? How quickly would we learn to reproduce such "primitive" tools as woven fish weirs, birch bark canoes, and chipped quartz arrowheads?

I stopped to fish two or three times during the day. So far, I had caught five trout: yesterday's brookie in Chemquasabamticook Stream, one today while trolling in light rapids, and the others when I paused to fish in some riffles. The lakes seemed to yield little. No trout reached the legal keeper limit of ten inches.

At 5:30 in the evening, I beached some two miles upstream from the bridge, which in turn is two miles upstream from Round Pond, where I planned to spend the night. One or two casts and I hooked a trout. Two casts later, I missed a second, so I settled for a dinner of one ultra-fresh trout and a can of spaghetti with meatballs. I pushed on and ran shallow rapids in the half light of the evening, thinking I would reach the pond shortly. I realized this was not to be when the bridge appeared. Round Pond and the next camping site were yet two miles on. I paddled in the serenity of the coming gloaming. At the delta above Round Pond, an elm stood in solitary splendor, at attention, saluting me as I passed. With the twilight darkening, two Canadian sentinels honked at my arrival. They had staked claim to a private island the size of a golf green for their nest. They were determined to drive me off by sheer noise. Farther along, another lone elm saluted. Elms? I must check my tree book when at home. What do elms do this far north?

Finally, I cleared the delta, and Round Pond created space and air. A gorgeous pond with tranquil hills dressed in spruce. In the morning I would see a guide camp, meet the waterway ranger, and speak to a pair of day fishermen in a motorized canoe. But this evening, I beached at Inlet camping area in solitude. There was just time to pitch my tent in the mostly dark and creep into my sleeping bag. The loons immediately launched into an evening symphony. No, not a lullaby. More a Wagnerian Götterdämmerung, with Valkyries alternately screaming, moaning, sighing, calling, conversing, and laughing. With the loons in full voice, solitude for one night.

16 May 1998

Yes, elusive is the object of my search. No sooner found, it melts from view as does a desert mirage. At early rising, I pushed off in the canoe for a few good morning casts. Casts to welcome the day. A hit would have been appreciated, but catching a fish was not the purpose of putting into the lake at that hour. Hardly started, I was startled by a beached canoe north of my camp. I turned instantly and fished to the south with a point obscuring the canoe. Out of sight, but not out of mind. My search was once again obstructed.

Despite the intrusion, Round Pond is recommended. As one might infer from its name, the pond appears circular in shape from the shore, although it is not circular at all. It could be a child's cutout of the *Niña* or the *Pinta*, or of Drake's *Golden Hind*, without the sails and masts, and with an exaggerated rudder. From the Inlet camping area, one can just make out on the far shore, a mile or so away, a guide camp. The beached canoe, it turned out, marked the Waterway ranger's hut. The other signs of man are the seven campsites scattered at various points along the shore. The pond is ringed by pleasant hills. Spruce is the predominant species of tree. The water is clear. An idyllic spot. As I dallied over morning coffee, the ranger's outboard motor erased the murmuring of bird songs and the whisper of the breeze in the trees. The object of my search, despite the beauty of the setting, was not to be found here.

The ranger came ashore. A younger version of the Katharine Hepburn who played opposite Humphrey Bogart in *The African Queen*. Tanned. Wrinkled. A quick smile. Disheveled. Old jeans, plaid shirt, green-vested life jacket, cap, boots. A twinkle in blue eyes. Well-worn, but worn well. I suppressed the surprise that rose in me. Why shouldn't a woman do such work? Much safer here, after all, than the life of a social worker in downtown Philadelphia or northeast Washington DC. We chatted.

Her enthusiasm, her obvious enjoyment of these woods and her life were infectious. She spends six months each year on the pond, starting May 1. Two weeks in, then two days out. She had "come in," she said, the afternoon before with two weeks of groceries and was fussing with a broken gas refrigerator. She registered me, told me it would be just over twenty dollars if I spent four nights. I would need to submit my receipt to the Waterway ranger at Michaud Farm on the west bank some four miles upstream from Allagash Falls. The ranger there would warn me about the falls, although anyone descending the Allagash ignorant of the falls would be wise not to travel far from the comfort of his TV and couch. The ranger also, she said, would recommend that I portage around the forty-foot drop. Not bad advice.

While I was fumbling in my rucksack for the twenty dollars I needed to pay, a boat with outboard motor and two men roared up and beached. The four of us exchanged good days. The two were local men, off to the Allagash for a day of fishing. They had put in at the bridge just above Round Pond. We discussed a meeting the men had attended the evening before. The Maine State Legislature was considering legislation to further protect the Allagash Wilderness Waterway. Hearings were being held at towns surrounding the waterway. The ranger asked how the meeting had gone.

The issues were important and diverse. Protection of the Waterway's beauty, of its fish and wildlife and flora. The rights of the lumber companies that own the land to earn a return on their investment: that is, to cut, transport, and plant trees, and, potentially, to develop or sell the land. Access to the Waterway by local residents who by tradition were permitted to enjoy the fishing, hunting, camping, and hiking the region offers, and who pay local taxes that they believe entitle them to these enjoyments. The desire of nonresidents such as myself to visit the Waterway, which some consider a national resource. And the interest of the State Legislature in attracting tourist dollars for the motels, the guides, the merchants, and others who benefit from the tourist trade.

The Allagash Wilderness Waterway was established in 1966 by the Maine Legislature. Development, construction, or cutting is prohibited within five hundred feet of the Waterway, the area owned by the state of Maine. Cause needs to be shown before permission can be granted for any such activity within two thousand feet of the Waterway. Timber harvesting within a mile of the high-water mark is conducted in accordance with a plan approved by the state. No access roads or trails, in addition to those already existing in 1966, are permitted. Camping is limited to designated sites and to "low-impact" camping—no cutting of trees or shrubs, no fires except in fireplaces at campsites, all waste to be carried out. Everyone entering the Waterway must register. Fees may be levied.

Establishment of the Waterway cast a net of protection over the Allagash. It also created a surge in visitors. Use is estimated at 50,000 visitor nights May through September. The Maine Legislature is considering tightening regulations. Possibilities include limiting the number of access points and banning motorized craft (motorboats in summer, snowmobiles in winter). Locals are generally against such restrictions, which would limit their use of the Waterway. The restrictions, in their view, favor the yuppie nonresident conservationist recreationalist over the pragmatic resident sportsman. Their tongue-in-cheek solution to preserve the Waterway is to limit nonresidents to canoes with paddles, and to restrict their trespass to a one-way southerly direction. That is, upstream. However, they and every other thinking person realize that increased use of the Waterway, whether by locals or transients, threatens the Waterway and decreases the pleasure of those who come here.

I pushed off from the Inlet at high noon. On passing the ranger camp, I paused to inquire about the spring a bit farther along. (It announced itself on my map as "built" by a Maine guide. Was that Willard Jalbert?) Was the water potable? The ranger said some who tried drinking it had had bad results, but perhaps this early in the season…? Despite the warning, I filled my water bottles at the spring.

The Round Pond Rips roared loudly but did not offer much bite. Halfway through, I turned into a backwater behind a boulder in the river. The canoe trapped itself as I fished. It was curious to sit so utterly becalmed in the tiny backwater while water roared and thrashed all around. Whenever the canoe drifted a few feet, threatening to flee into the raging current, the maelstrom gently nudged it back into the pool of calm like a loving mother, protecting it from the storm of whitewater waves. Might I one day develop the wisdom to evince the serenity of such a tranquil backwater when life's tumult batters 'round me.

Below the Rips, at Turk Island campground, the boat and the two fishermen I had seen earlier in the day had been joined by a second boat. The four fishermen were exchanging views on the efficacy of their respective outboard motors. I was surprised to hear, in these deep Maine woods, the praise heaped by one of the owners on his Yamaha. A Yamaha? Was Maine not as parochial as Congress perennially tended to believe? Whatever happened to Evinrude and Mercury?

Below the Rips, another mile or two of current and gentle rapids. The water was low. The Round Pond fishermen claimed it was the lowest water they had seen in May in their fifty years on the Allagash. And then came two or three miles of still black water known as the Musquocook Deadwater. Aptly named. Dreary. Foreboding. Absent of distinguishing features. Somewhere above this stretch, I had stopped and caught a small trout. At Musquocook Stream, I stopped again. Fished near its mouth. No hits. Hardly there and a canoe with two male paddlers passed me. They planned to camp, they said, at Five Finger East. I had intended to stay at the campsite across the river at Five Finger West. Given their presence, I would seek farther.

Shortly after they passed me, I stopped again to fish, this time at Five Finger Brook, upriver from the two Five Finger campsites. Within a few minutes, I had landed five brook trout. All savage. All fighters. None more than seven inches in length. A joy to hook, to play, to meet. And a joy to release. Instead of trout, I heated a can of beef stew on the bank of this happy stream, which leapt joyfully into the Allagash, only to lose its gaiety in the dreary stretch of Deadwater.

Later, I passed Five Finger East in silence, without being remarked. Paddling without a sound, no bang of paddle on gunwale, no slurp of water to betray me. I took childish pride in the furtive passage.

After sundown but in the yet bright light of the early gloaming, I reached Pelletier Deadwater South. I scouted it. Walked the hundred yards downstream to Pelletier Deadwater North. Distinctly preferable. High on the bank, a small open area for my tent and furnished with a permanent picnic table. Moreover, in these high latitudes, when seeking solitude, north is *a priori* preferable to south. As I pitched camp, a moose appeared across the river. He hesitated at the sight of my canoe. The second moose I had seen that day. He crossed the river toward me, intending, it would seem, to share a drink and a chat with me. Big fellow. Bull. Ragged hair. No rack showing yet. It would be growing shortly. He splashed through the water, ten or twelve inches deep, for the hundred yards from the small island. Picking his way slowly. Even with his four legs, the stones in the river made for an awkward gait. All legs and, like a teenage boy, all joints. Each leg seemed to have tens of articulations. Locomotion for a moose is an anagram of moving parts. Curious how in the woods they can cover ground so quickly when they run. Across he came, then seemed to disdain his earlier thought of joining me for a drink and followed the shoreline upstream.

Come first light, he would be again on the opposite shore, would again gaze thoughtfully at my canoe, again amble across, this time apparently to share a morning cup of coffee.

Night crept on the river as I sipped from a small flask, all the while listening and watching. After I had drunk my fill of the night sounds, I slept soundly. Morning was quiet, for a while. Then flotillas of canoes. At half-hour intervals: a man and a woman, a party of four, a party of eight. I will push off. It is the Saturday before the Memorial Day weekend. It may be time to abandon my search.

17 May 1998

An awful day yesterday. People. People. And more

people. They passed my camp in waves during the morning, a true invasion. Once I was on the water, another party of six passed me. At Michaud Farm Ranger Station and again at Allagash Falls portage, it was a county fair. People jostled, shouted greetings, milled about. Packages, boxes, packs, and gear were strewed about. Canoeists sweated and puffed as they carried their loads the quarter mile around the falls. Cameras were shared as groups took pictures of one another. It was all in good humor. There was laughter and cheer. Everyone was having fun, enjoying the crowd. A nuclear explosion could not have devastated my search more utterly.

One of the youngsters offered to help portage my canoe. I thanked him and mumbled that it was a point of honor to manage the carry without assistance. To accept his assistance would be to accept a failing grade for the trip. He was nonplussed. I noted with childish pleasure that I completed the portage more quickly than did the others, all of whom portaged in pairs. I didn't say it, but it is also a point of honor to travel light.

The roar of the falls drowned out the war cries of the invaders. I fished the turmoil and the froth, the raging current and waves, the powerful back currents below the thunder. The falls are said to be forty feet high. Not quite a straight drop, but a fury of pounding water and spray.

The paddle below the falls was no joy. For the next two hours, I was never out of sight of at least one other canoe; and often I could see two or three on the attack, sometimes ahead of me, sometimes behind. Camping sites were manned with the invaders until I put out at Big Brook North. Across the way, two canoes were beached at Big Brook East. The hammer of an ax on a tent pole, the bang of gear, the echo of instructions, carried to me. An invading legion was laying siege, preparing for battle.

I pitched my tent, cooked, and ate. There was hope that darkness would bring calm, allow solitude to creep around. It was not to be.

Voices. Banging of paddles. The rasp of a hull on rocks. They know the site is taken. My canoe is on the shore. Etiquette demands that one not intrude on an occupied campsite. There was, however, no denying that etiquette tonight would be breached. Fate had decried I would be defeated on this, my last night of the trip.

There were apologies. All sites upriver were occupied. Four canoes at Big Brook South. Two could be seen across the river at East. The next sites at Twin Brook were another four miles. Too far to go. Light almost faded. We regret. Sorry to impose.

I considered breaking camp, escaping into the night. Instead, I mumbled acceptance to the apologies, recognized their plight, bade them welcome, likened that I had intended to fish, and fled upstream in my canoe with my fly rod.

When dark settled in, I returned to the tent. My preferred option was to ignore the two invaders, zip up my tent, and go to sleep. It would not have worked. Their tent was pitched, but they were just launching battle with campfire, cookstove, and a plethora of pots and pans. The din of frenzied instructions, opening rucksacks, chopping wood, stacking and unstacking pots, and clanging their covers could be heard for miles up and down the river. My tent stood only fifteen feet away. Sleep was not an option.

If they can't be beat, join them, so enlist I did. We introduced ourselves. First names, no more. David and Brian. New Yorkers, complete with accent. Not from Brooklyn, but definitely New York. David blond and blue-eyed. A true Viking. The strong jaw that projects manhood. Broad shoulders, small waist. He chopped the wood, laid and lit the fire, swigged from a bottle of vodka. A man's man. A four-day growth of beard enhanced the image of the heroic woodsman.

Brian, on the other hand, was short. Very short. Overweight. Soft belly. Black hair too long, straggly, greasy. A bald spot on the top of his head. Flat round face with a big nose and protruding eyeballs. A full black beard. A Hasidic Jew who should be praying at the Wailing Wall, not playing at outdoorsman.

He cooked the meal. No, he prepared dinner. He proudly pointed out the high-tech cookware. A gas stove that unfurled like a flower, with pieces that snapped into place to efficiently reflect and redistribute heat. Tens of pots weighing mere ounces stacked into a minuscule carry case. A covered dish that acted as an oven when enveloped in a flameproof mitten. Freeze-dried meals no heavier than a handful of feathers in plastic bags guaranteed to keep for two decades. Clip the bag open, add water, massage for a minute or two, and pour into the pan. A three-course meal. Quiche as an appetizer, ravioli as the entrée, coffee cake for dessert. Cappuccino to finish. Our astronauts could learn from these two what *high-tech* means.

With the coffee, out came the pipes. Raised eyebrows at my polite refusal. I explained that I was leery even to swallow an aspirin. No comprehension. And then they brought out more serious stuff. Further disbelief when I refused to taste the mushrooms, but I was unable to escape a discourse on their astronomical price, exceptional purity, size/shape/color upon harvesting, their origin in California, and the superiority of their effect over marijuana, heroin, cocaine, peyote, or any other drug.

David and Brian “did” a river each year. The trip was, well, a trip, its essence derived from the particularly high-quality drugs procured over the month preceding the trip. As the wood fire burned itself out and the fires within glowed hot, David and Brian retired, amorously, to their tent. At 4 a.m., first light, I left. Never had I broken camp so silently or quickly. It is impossible to load a canoe and slide it off rocks into a river without a splash or a bang or a knock. That morning it was done.

By 4:15 I was on the water, dipping my oar with the silence of a gliding owl. The half darkness enveloped me. When I was two hundred yards downriver and around the bend, I pulled at my paddle in a frenzy. I had been defeated, but I was alive. If I could flee the field of battle quickly, I might yet live to take another trip into the wilds, to search again for solitude. To win this war.

18 May 1998

Calm succeeds the storm of battle. So it was on this, my last hours on the Allagash. Due to my early departure, and because no one was camped downstream, the last three hours did bring solace, if not the deep solitude I sought. The light mist on the river dissipated with the rising sun. The world was at peace. The current ran more swiftly here, so I hardly paddled. A few strokes now and again on the flats to provide direction. Mostly I drifted, satisfied to let the current do the work. The previous day, with other canoes constantly in view, my reaction had been to paddle hard, to keep pace with the crowd. A reaction I tried to stifle more than once, but it was difficult to control. So it goes on the job, living in the city, or driving on the interstate to work. Our lives are pulled along by a social force field, as invisible as gravity, undeniable in its strength. Solitude delivers us from this force field, but the void frightens those who have no internal force field of their own.

On those last miles that morning, there were a number of rapids. Choppy water, swiftness, but only a few rocks to avoid. The last hundred yards, just above the sign announcing I was "Leaving Allagash Wilderness Waterway," stretched a run of the fastest water of the day. A run of chop and speed seemingly created to emphasize the notice on the sign. A fitting adieu. One might hope one's life ended with such a stretch of rapids. Clearly in control of the canoe, with the current boiling clean and swift.

In the morning calm, I beached the canoe to breakfast on fiddlehead ferns. They grow in profusion along the length of the Waterway and are just perfect for eating at this time of year. The unfurled tips of the fern are tender and sweet. Some boil them; others eat them with salad dressing. Having no oil, vinegar, mustard, or salt and pepper to concoct a vinaigrette, I simply ate them raw. Delicious if at the right stage. When tightly furled, they are too young, spoiled by a fuzz still within them. If largely unfurled, they stiffen and lose their flavor. At the half-furled stage, the fuzz has disappeared, and the remaining bud is at its most delectable. I grazed as a deer might, wandering the bank, selecting amongst the thousands of buds only those at the perfect stage. I could imagine a small party of Indians on this journey five thousand years ago, gathering these fiddleheads by the basketful.

The Indians had a hard life. Do not romanticize it. But at times of abundance, they lived well. Imagine roasted grouse, broiled venison, wild blueberries, boiled maple syrup, fresh trout, crisp watercress. Oh, yes, and imagine long winter storms with bitter cold, driving snow, a howling wind, and nothing to eat but a few strings of frozen pemmican. Their lives brought both joy and sorrow, as do ours. Our measure of each derives from within, not from the fickle smiles or frowns of Fortune, as we tend to believe when winter winds howl. Our portions of joy and sorrow vary neither from era to era, nor from nation to nation. They vary only by individual, dependent solely on our dispositions.

At the Twin Brook Luncheonette in Allagash Village, I beached the canoe one last time. Since breaking camp three hours earlier, I had seen no one. A pleasant last run. I telephoned Sean Lizotte, my guide, who had promised to pick me up. A cup of coffee and talk at the counter was my gateway back into civilization. Kelly Lizotte with her two young ones in tow arrived shortly to drive me to my car. Back at the house, Sean and I talked grouse. The best time is the second and third weeks of October. The grouse are in the apples, the leaves are off the trees, the deer season is still closed. Sean has two dogs. The pointer is young and wild, but the Weimaraner hunts close, he says, necessary for grouse. Room, board, dog, and guide would be $450 per week. I am drawn to return to continue my search in October.

The canoe on the car, the gear in the trunk, I headed first east to Fort Kent, then south to Bangor. Two hundred miles to Bangor where civilization begins. Three hundred twenty to Portland, four hundred twenty to Boston. (Some might claim it's ten thousand miles from Boston. Who am I to argue?). The northern tip of Maine is well north of the forty-fifth parallel, which to the west forms the border between Canada and Vermont and New York, and north as well of Montreal and the city of Quebec.

The drive down Route 11 and Interstate 95 eased me back into today's world. The radio informed me that Frank Sinatra had died. That the last performance of Seinfeld had aired. That David Wells had pitched a perfect game in Yankee Stadium against the Twins. Dandelions were still a startling yellow in the green pastures. Mauve flowers bloomed in the bogs. There was little traffic as I cruised I95. Though solitude had eluded me, peace reigned over the northern wilderness.

LOST

Snow sifted through the hemlocks, hissing against the needles, quieting the darkening woods. The brown needles underfoot showed as dark tufts through the thin cover of white. Dan looked hard toward where the ground sloped downward to form a small glade. There were no hemlocks there, just scrub oak fighting for space. He looked but did not let his eyes focus. He looked for movement, for a patch of misplaced color.

His eyes stung. Even the gray of the glade was dark. Under the trees, it was nearly too dark to shoot. Dan pushed up from the ground and leaned his rifle against the hemlock he had used for a backrest, placing the butt in the brown patch of needles where he had been sitting. He had to watch his hands to remove his mittens; his hands were cold, the mittens stiff. He pushed them into a pocket and loosened his belt, slid both hands down inside his pants to his crotch, tensing as cold met hot. His hands seared from the heat. The pain lessened slowly as his hands warmed.

Damn, he thought. He'd expected to have better luck. It had been cold, must have been nearly ten below at first light. It felt even colder now. He had sat here in the early morning waiting for the dawn to come, thinking that in the scrub below he would see a deer. Two trails met there, and a little farther down he had found a bed. After dawn he had had to get up, needing to move because of the cold. He had drifted along the edge of the glade, keeping under the hemlocks where he didn't make much noise. He had hoped to jump a deer. Hoping against hope. There had been no snow to track; and unless he was in the hemlocks, it was noisy underfoot. But it had been too cold for an all-day stand; and anyway, the deer wouldn't have been moving. Too cold and too noisy.

But he'd had a feeling this morning. An exultance. A sureness that today he would get a shot. He smiled wryly. He had that feeling every morning.

After starting and stopping all day, with a lot more stopping than starting, he had returned to this spot overlooking the glade before heading home. It was the last day of the season. He judged it had started snowing an hour ago. It was, he thought, all over. No deer this year.

He breathed into his mittens before putting them on. Time to head out. A half hour and it would be dark. He cradled the rifle in the crook of his left arm, cupping his right hand around the trigger guard to avoid some branch snagging the trigger and firing the gun. He checked to see that the hammer was in the half-cocked position. On safety.

He traveled along the edge of the glade, stopping every few yards to listen to the hiss of the snow and to peer under the dark hemlocks and across the scrub oak. He looked back along his path to see that his footprints were visible in the just fallen snow. Nowhere a sound. The world extended only a few yards in every direction, beyond the whiteness, or blackness, depending on whether he looked across the scrub oak or under the pines.

He moved faster now for it was getting darker. Then

tracks! Even in the thin layer of white, he saw immediately that it was a deer going from the glade of scrub to the pines. He paused before swinging along the track. It was dark, but then it was only a half mile to the house, and even in the dark he could get home from here. This section he had hunted a hundred times. And the track was fresh. My God, it was fresh! It was snowing, but there was no snow in the prints. Perhaps a minute or two behind him. Large prints, must be a buck. Probably the one Wayne said he missed last week.

Slowly, boy, slowly. Stop and listen. Look. Move on and stop again. He twisted and turned, slipping through the brush of the glade, gaze glued to the tracks in the snow. After a few minutes he slid his right mitten off and into a pocket. Just in case. Straining his eyes, looking without focusing. Then excitement grabbed him like two fists, one throttling his throat, the other smashing into his stomach. He froze. Behind him, not more than ten yards, a twig had snapped. Adrenaline surged. He froze, forced the excitement down into his belly, quieted himself. Slowly, he turned his head and shoulders, his thumb on the hammer, readying for a shot.

Steady, boy, steady.

But it was too dark. He looked. He waited. No sound, nothing to see. But it had not been his imagination. Not ten yards! Hard to outwait a deer, but he would do it. Five minutes, ten. Twenty minutes. Only the whisper of the snow.

He had to move. Even at ten yards, he couldn't shoot now. Way too dark. Dan pushed one foot out and shifted his weight. Again, the muscles in throat and belly bunched. Right there where he was looking, another twig had snapped. The deer had outwaited him. Eyes straining to see, he walked toward the spot. Nothing. Looking down, he saw he had been right. Not fifteen yards from where he had frozen was the evidence. The deer tracks on top of his back trail. So, the deer had been following him. Smart bastard. Dan turned toward home. Nearly got him, he thought. But it had been too late and too dark. Hard to believe he hadn't been able to see the deer at all at that distance.

He'd hardly gone fifty yards when he saw tracks again. This time a man's. Hadn't heard anyone in here. Wait! They were his own. No, couldn't be his own: he hadn't been here. Carefully, he measured, inspected the tread of the print. There was no doubt; they were his. How could it be? He hadn't been here, he reiterated to himself. But they were his. He slowed his breathing, forced himself to relax, to deal with that momentary surge of panic. When panic grips, he reminded himself, stop. Stop, pause, and when you are quieted, decide what to do.

He leaned the rifle against a tree and took off his mitten, felt in his coat pocket. Good. He had matches. Nothing to worry about. He didn't want to stay out all night, but he could if he had to. His wife would worry, and it wouldn't be any fun in this cold, but there was no danger. He need only to build a fire and avoid falling asleep.

Okay, now that he didn't have to worry, what should he do? He thought back along his trail, trying to remember where he might have gotten confused. Must have been while following the deer. But that didn't help. He had been too sure of where he was. He was positive he hadn't been here. But he had. So, he was lost.

Backtracking was not possible; it was snowing too fast. Build a fire or take a direction first? Better not walk, he thought. Fall into a stream and get wet and he'd be in a hell of a fix. It was only a half mile back to the house. No problem. No problem unless he walked in the wrong direction. The next road in the wrong direction was thirty miles across woods, a swamp, and a river.

Perhaps if he listened, he'd hear something. A truck, a car's horn. Somebody calling, a dog barking. He listened. Waited. The snow swished. It shouldn't snow when it was so cold; it was only supposed to snow when it was warming up. He shook his shoulders and arms, jogged in place without lifting his feet from the ground. Have to start a fire soon. And then, above the hiss of snow on needles he heard another hiss, a soft, dull drone. A car passing on the road. Within a few seconds, the sound was gone.

He cradled the rifle in the crook of his left arm, cupped his right hand about the trigger guard. Checked to see that the hammer was in the half-cocked position, on safety. He moved off in the direction of the sound. His wife would be worried, upset that his dinner would be cold.

A STRANGE TALE

A number of years ago, a strange tale was whispered in the dark streets of La Paz, Bolivia. How much of the tale is true is difficult to know, for we are all aware how stories blossom and grow. Yet there is no doubt that George Hayes and his wife left La Paz to hunt in the mountains north of Lake Titicaca, and that he returned alone. She was never seen again. That much of the story is fact, and who knows, therefore, how much of the remainder is fact as well? Have not stranger events, equally dubious tales, stories no one initially believed, eventually been proven to be true?

George Hayes and his wife Maria had come to La Paz for the first time. They had traveled over much of the world together, for George Hayes was wealthy. Not having to work for a living, he had the money and the time for leisure. As a diversion, he had decided early on to become a hunter. He and Maria had spent their ten years of marriage hunting game in the mountains and jungles of the various continents. He not only became a famous big-game hunter, but the guides he employed all admired his marksmanship, although some raised questions as to his stamina and courage. On more than one occasion, he declined to push into thick brush to finish off a wounded lion or wild buffalo. He was a tall blond man with blue eyes and an even tan on his face, and most people found him easy to like. Although he came from a rich New York family, he did not try to impress people with either his wealth or his heritage.

George Hayes and Maria were happy together. He was a kind husband who showered his spouse with flowers and baubles, and she was a model wife. Since he liked to travel, they had decided not to have children, but rather to enjoy themselves and their freedom.

She was a beautiful woman, and her dark hair and slight figure matched with his blond coloring and tall frame made them a handsome couple. Everyone agreed that were they to decide to have children, those children would be exquisite.

As one might infer, the Hayeses had come to La Paz to hunt. George Hayes had heard that near Lake Titicaca, there were mountain sheep and a sort of mountain lion, both of which are difficult game to shoot; and Maria thought La Paz would be an interesting town. While George inquired about the hunting, they stayed in La Paz. The two of them walked about the city or played golf during the day; at night, they dined and enjoyed the gay life.

This visit was much like all their trips, for soon after being married, both George and Maria discovered what pleased the other most. George found that Maria enjoyed traveling and exploring new cities; she found that he enjoyed hunting. So, each decided to cultivate an interest in the other's pleasure: Maria took up shooting while George was mindful to spend a few weeks of leisure in some foreign city before and after each hunting expedition. In this way, they both agreed, their life was full and varied.

While in La Paz preparing their equipment and inquiring for guides, George Hayes met an old wizened man who had lived as a boy in the Mt. Sorata region. It was exactly this region where George Hayes wished to hunt—north of Lake Titicaca, wild and mountainous, and renowned for its mountain lions and sheep. At first, the old man would give no information about this desolate terrain. He even seemed frightened. Then he begged George Hayes not to hunt north of Lake Titicaca, especially not near Mt. Sorata, and especially not to take his wife. When pressured, the old man blurted out a vague story of a fierce mountain tribe.

When George Hayes tried to reconstruct the story for his wife, he could not tell her whether the mountain tribe was composed of savage men or gigantic beasts or half of each; whether it was fact or fiction or if the tribe had ever been seen or not. All he had understood was that the region was uninhabited because men feared the mountain tribe, whatever it was, and that the fear stemmed largely from a belief that the tribe kidnapped beautiful women. One fact had seemed clear: the women, whether carried off or lost, were always beautiful and always childless. It was for this reason that the old man had warned George Hayes not to go. Wasn't his wife beautiful? And childless? But George Hayes had laughed at the old man. As a hunter, he had heard fantastic stories that rarely had a basis in fact, and even then were wildly exaggerated. He was amused by this legend, partly like the yeti he had been warned about when hunting in Tibet; partly seven brides for seven brothers; and partly the sea monster of the Scottish lochs. How many times had a widely feared man-eating lion or indomitable African buffalo been described as monstrous, enormous, ferocious by local villagers only to shrink, once shot, to hardly larger than the norm?

George Hayes did not find it hard to persuade himself and his beautiful wife that they had nothing to fear. It would have been better, perhaps, if the two of them had heeded the old man's warning.

Preparations for the expedition continued, and in a few weeks George Hayes and Maria and a small party left La Paz. The group traveled to Lake Titicaca by truck over rough gravel roads, then hiked northward through the Andes to the Peru-Bolivia border. The land was wild and lonely, but magnificent. Both George Hayes and Maria admitted that nowhere had they seen a land such as this. George Hayes was convinced that the hunting would be superb; his wife was enthralled with the majesty of the Andes. Even before they reached their main camp, they were certain their trip would be a success.

After trekking for the better part of a fortnight, the party came to the banks of a river where it flowed quietly through a grassy glade. The glade was lovelier than any of the previous camping spots, with the quiet river, the lush grass, and Mt. Sorata seeming to rise vertically from their feet. They immediately decided they would establish their base camp here. The tents were pitched, the food was stored in canvas bags hung from tree limbs, canvas cots were erected, a fire pit was built, and soon the camp was a tidy, comfortable settlement. The next morning, George Hayes and his wife began to hunt, and it took no time to prove game to be abundant on the slopes of Mt. Sorata.

During the first week, they spotted many wild sheep but shot just three. George Hayes cleanly killed a trophy ram while his wife shot two smaller ones. Having bagged his trophy ram, George Hayes wanted to try for a mountain lion. His wife and all but one guide would remain in camp; it would be easier for a small party to stalk the prey.

George Hayes and the guide set out in the morning and did not return until late afternoon. As they neared the campsite, they heard shouting. Something was amiss. They sprinted toward the glade, where the cook and bearers clustered about the Hayeses' tent. George Hayes did not see his wife and was afraid she had been hurt, but on reaching the tent he saw that she was not within. Everybody was talking, and only after silencing all but the cook did George Hayes learn what had happened. Mrs. Hayes, the cook said, had stepped into the tent only ten minutes before to freshen up for her husband's return. Moments later, the bearers and cook heard her scream, but the scream did not come from the tent. It came from across the river. On racing to the tent, they found it empty. How Mrs. Hayes had left the tent, no one could explain. The tent stood in the very center of the glade, and though everyone had seen her enter, everyone swore she had not exited.

It did not take George Hayes and the guide long to find the mark of a footprint, ostensibly that of a man, near the river; and on the opposite bank, another footprint where he had climbed from the water. There was no trace of a smaller print that might belong to Maria. They swiftly followed the spoor but were forced to abandon it once night fell. George Hayes returned to camp. He was furious. He could not understand how so many men could have let his wife be abducted from under their very noses. And there was no doubt that this is what happened.

One by one, George Hayes called the bearers into his tent, and one by one, he grilled them. Always the story was the same: Mrs. Hayes had entered the tent, could not have left, but had screamed from somewhere across the river. No one had been seen. Only the cook had something further to add. His father had lived near Lake Titicaca as a boy and had heard tales of a wild and ferocious tribe comprised—in his version of the story—of creatures who were half man, half beast. These ferocious beasts were alleged to kidnap women. But not just any women. The women, his father had said, were always beautiful and always without child. Until now, the cook had not believed the stories, but it made one wonder… especially when Mrs. Hayes was beautiful and childless…

George Hayes was enraged and threw the cook out of the tent.

The next morning, George Hayes and the guide struck out on the spoor, following it from the river as they had the night before. George Hayes was convinced his wife had been abducted, and he was determined to find her. Although his guide was an excellent tracker, the man or beast or whatever it had been had left an intricate trail and finally no trail at all. George Hayes and the guide returned to camp. George Hayes was fuming at having lost the spoor, but he had no intention of giving up the search.

That evening, he called the cook back to his tent and asked politely for any details he might recall about the wild and ferocious tribe. George Hayes was now convinced that the man, or creature, that had abducted his wife was no ordinary being. The trail had been too complex, too convoluted. Thus, determined as he was to leave no stone unturned, and as the stories of the tribe of half men, half beast were his only clue, George Hayes asked the cook for any information he might have.

The cook was garrulous, but his information was

scanty. George Hayes could only gather that if such a tribe existed, it dwelled somewhere in the wilderness near or north of Mt. Sorata. George Hayes vowed silently that he would not leave the area until he had searched every crevice and gulley of the Andes.

The next day, George Hayes sent the bearers and the cook back to La Paz and struck out with the guide to begin the search. For days, the two of them combed the ragged peaks and tree-filled valleys, but nowhere was there a sign of any human life. The Andes were beautiful and game was plentiful, but in this wilderness, George Hayes despaired of ever finding his wife. Yet he continued the search.

The days dragged on until one morning, George Hayes and the guide found a mountain stream they had not noticed before. They followed the stream toward its source, as much out of curiosity as in hope of finding a clue as to the whereabouts of Maria. But then George Hayes noticed that what he had assumed was a game trail along the bank of the stream did not have the random twists and turns most game trails had. He could not say why, but to him the trail seemed to have more purpose, as if it were a human pathway. Yet it was seldom used, judging by the brush along the sides, and there were no signs of human passage. George Hayes had nearly given up this theory when, at a falls, they stood before a rock face and saw steps hewed out of the stone, leading up. George Hayes and the guide stood stupefied before the steps. Slowly, George Hayes realized that this path, these stairs, must be the remnants of an Indian civilization, Aztec perhaps, more probably Inca. Perhaps the path led to a temple nestled in a cave or a ruined city high on the mountain. George Hayes and the guide studied the steps for a few minutes, then ascended and pushed on along the stream.

The path along the stream was much as before, but often on the steep, rocky slopes they found more steps hewn from the rock. Finally, George Hayes and the guide reached a cliff that towered hundreds of feet above them. The stream they had been following cascaded in white mist from the very top. They searched the rock face and found a stairway leading up. After pausing to catch their breath, they pushed on. It was a long climb up, the steps worn by weather or, perhaps, by the soles of thousands of feet. Then the steps led into the cliff and spiraled upward in the dark of a cave, more a chimney or a well than a cave. Around and around they went, as if in a castle turret, before bursting finally into the sunlight.

George Hayes and the guide had left the world below and stood in a valley cupped in the crater of a long-extinct volcano. The valley was a sparkling green emerald in the sun, lush with grass and dotted with patches of woods. The silver ribbon of the stream meandered toward where the stairs emerged and then flowed through a gorge to fall to the world below. The slopes that rose from the floor of the valley were heavily forested with handsome pines; the lush grass was flecked with the white of grazing sheep; and above the ridge around the valley, the sky was blue and here and there, a farther peak of the Andes glistened with snow. The valley was serene in the sun, warm and fertile and green.

All this was amazing to George Hayes, but even more amazing was the cluster of stone buildings crawling up the slope at the head of the valley. George Hayes had hiked years before to Machu Picchu. These buildings reminded him of that visit, all precise stonework and breathtaking views, an Eden in the mountains. If it was not an Inca ruin from the fifteenth century, a restored lost village, then it had been built by offspring of those forgotten architects.

As George Hayes and the guide gaped at the beautiful and fertile valley, two bronzed and handsome men appeared. The men were unarmed, so George Hayes waited for them to come near. He was amazed when the men greeted him in Castilian. George Hayes returned the greeting, and as the men seemed friendly, he inquired if this was where they lived. They told him they lived in the village at the head of the valley, that the flocks of sheep and goats belonged to the villagers, and that the tilled fields also were theirs. Then George Hayes explained that the guide and he were searching for his wife and asked if the men had any information that would aid them in their search. They answered that they had no information, but invited George Hayes and the guide to come to the village and put their questions to their chief.

The four men started for the head of the valley, following a path along the stream. The stream alternately flowed under cool trees and through open glades, between cultivated fields of rich loam and grassy meadows where goats and sheep grazed peacefully. It was a fertile, idyllic valley, and as they walked, the guide exclaimed ecstatically that never had he seen such healthy livestock or luxuriant crops. He asked the two men if there was game in the valley. They answered that the pine forests on the slopes of the old crater sheltered many deer, which the villagers hunted, but that it had been several years since a mountain lion had lived in the valley. The guide asked why. Did not the deer and livestock attract them? The two men answered that there was only one entrance to the crater that surrounded the valley, the stairway they had found. It was rare for a mountain lion to enter the valley. When they'd had one years ago, the villagers had hunted and killed him.

As the four men reached the cluster of buildings, George Hayes saw at once that his first impression was right: this was an Incan retreat. The streets and houses were built of hand-quarried stone, perhaps centuries old. He was thunderstruck. How could such an idyllic spot be unknown to the civilized world? As the four men entered the village, men and women and children gathered to watch the two strangers. The people were handsome and healthy and seemed uncommonly happy. It was a remarkable village and a remarkable race.

The two men told George Hayes that the building they were approaching, with terraces and gardens about it, was where they would meet their chief. George Hayes asked his name. One of the men replied, but George Hayes did not catch the Spanish name.

For the first time in many years, George Hayes was off-balance, with no idea where he was or what he was seeing or how he should act. He had thought he'd find a ferocious tribe of crazed wild men, and it appeared he had found a lost civilization, or perhaps more correctly, a lost village. The chief received him graciously and set him at ease. He was no ferocious beast but simply a man, as handsome as his compatriots; stockier than the rest of his people; and obviously powerful, broad in the shoulder and barrel chested, but polite of manner and precise in his speech.

George Hayes and the chief spoke courteously on various subjects: hunting and fishing, farming and the beauty of the valley. George Hayes told of the mountain lions he had shot and showed the chief his gun. The chief had heard tell of guns but had never seen one. Nor had he ever killed a mountain lion. He noted there was no need of guns in the valley, given that there were no lions. The small talk went on until George Hayes deemed it was time to inquire about his wife. The chief casually replied that he had kidnapped Maria Hayes. He spoke as if such a kidnapping was nothing more than spotting an attractive pebble in a streambed, picking it up, and putting it in his pocket.

There was a pause as George Hayes composed himself, for he was astounded by the chief's cool avowal. After an awkward silence, George Hayes politely requested the return of his wife. The chief equally politely declined the demand. He stated that Maria Hayes was now a citizen of the valley and, moreover, was soon to be his wife. At this, George Hayes lost his temper and insisted on seeing his wife. To his surprise, the chief readily agreed.

On her arrival in the room, Maria rushed to her husband's side and tearfully embraced him. She was as beautiful as ever, perhaps more so, since she flushed happily at seeing her husband again. When she calmed down, he asked her how she had been treated during the past few weeks. She replied that the people of the valley had been most kind, that she had not felt at all a captive but more like a guest, a queen even. They were a wonderful people, she told him, kind and intelligent and happy, and the valley was exquisite. Everyone tilled the fields each morning, and the afternoons and evenings were devoted to household chores, making and repairing tools and clothes, cooking, tending the livestock, harvesting. All the work of a subsistence living. Life was simple and happy, and she was learning skills she had hardly known existed: spinning, weaving, beekeeping, shearing sheep, and the like, but she was overjoyed to be reunited with her husband. Glancing from her husband to the chief, she suddenly realized from the latter's demeanor that her husband's arrival did not mean she was free to leave the valley. She threw her arms around her husband and started to cry again.

George Hayes turned to the chief. This time he did not ask but insisted on the return of his wife. The chief shook his head. George Hayes exploded, demanded to know why the chief, who otherwise was so well-bred and intelligent, felt justified in kidnapping. The chief replied calmly that his valley always experienced a shortage of women; and to provide wives for all the men of his tribe, he abducted women from time to time. As he wished his people to be handsome and healthy, he only abducted beautiful women; and as he wanted the women to be happy in his valley, he never took any with children, for then their hearts pined for their little ones.

George Hayes protested and pointed to his tearful wife. The chief dismissed the tears, insisting that in a few months, the woman would be happy in the valley and would not want to leave. He invited George Hayes to return in a year's time and see. If his wife wanted to leave then, he would be free to take her.

George Hayes continued to protest vehemently. To calm him, the chief proposed a compromise. He would give his guest a chance to win his wife's freedom—they would see who could be the first to track and kill a mountain lion. They discussed the terms. George Hayes could use his gun, but not his guide. The chief would use his bow and would also hunt alone. The first to kill and carry home a mountain lion would be the victor. Should George Hayes win, he and his wife would be free to leave the valley. Should the chief win, Maria would remain in the valley for one year. At the end of that year, George Hayes could return and see for himself that his wife was happy and no longer wanted to leave.

George Hayes agreed. It was a fair contest.

The next day at dawn, the two men descended the steps together to the outer world. The villagers gathered to watch them depart, and they returned to the steps after they had worked in the fields. In the late afternoon, a man could be heard coming up the stairs. From the slow and heavy tread, it was apparent he carried a heavy burden. It was the village chief who emerged from the hole, a mountain lion on his shoulders. At dusk, George Hayes returned empty-handed. He had lost the contest and would have to wait one year before he could reclaim his wife. He departed the valley the next morning.

One year later, George Hayes returned to La Paz and hiked the wilderness north of Lake Titicaca by himself. He came to the village in the crater and was welcomed by the villagers. The valley was more beautiful than he remembered it, the grass lush and the fields rich, the sheep and goats peaceful in the meadows, and the ancient village, with the Andes rising high above it, magnificent. George Hayes and the chief spoke lightly on numerous topics, and finally the chief asked for George Hayes's wife to be sent in. As she entered the room, he left.

George Hayes stood opposite the woman, the two of them alone but for the infant she carried in her arms. She was more beautiful than his wife of a year before, a woman serene and fulfilled, happy as though she had some glorious secret all her own. She greeted George Hayes, and though he knew it was his wife, she seemed different from Maria. They spoke politely for a few minutes before George Hayes asked whether she wished to leave the valley. Already he knew her answer.

George Hayes was seen once more on his return to La Paz, and people remarked that though he seemed sad, he did not seem so disconsolate as a year before. He left La Paz a few days later and never returned to hunt for the mountain lion he had never shot. People found that strange, and who knows? Perhaps the story of the village in the mountains was invented to explain the disappearance of his wife and what many thought was his odd behavior.

SUNSET

The boy heard a car stop. Looking out the window, he saw the battered Buick had pulled up. He checked his watch: 4:45 p.m. The same as always. Always 4:45 p.m. Always the battered Buick with two other guys. And, as always, the old man who lived across the street opened the rear car door. He eased his legs off the seat and swung them out of the car. Carefully, he straightened, controlling his weight so as not to lose his balance. He nodded to the other two men, as he always did, closed the door, and took a step away from the car. The Buick drove off.

The boy continued to watch as the old man began the long journey to the house. Actually, it was not a long way from the road to the house—indeed, it was hardly five or six car lengths—but it always took the old man a long time.

Tom had lived here just a few weeks. He and his parents had moved onto Fall River Avenue just before school started. Every afternoon when he got back from school, he studied until dinnertime. His desk was up against his bedroom window, which looked out onto the street. Every weekday since they had lived here, he'd seen the old man come home.

Although Tom had never spoken to the old man, he felt sorry for him. The man had trouble walking, and he walked awkwardly, a staggered step-step. Maybe his right leg was wooden. More probably he was crippled, or possibly just old. He always went slowly, making sure he was balanced before taking each step.

He worked too, coming home as he did dressed in coveralls and a dirty plaid shirt. From the looks of him, he couldn't be doing physical labor. Tom figured he worked in a factory, an indoors job where he could sit down. It was kind of mean; it didn't seem right that a man that old should have to work.

But working wasn't the only reason Tom felt sorry for the old man. He lived with a family. The mother must be the old man's daughter. Or maybe the father was his son. Nobody paid much attention to the old man. Their three kids never even yelled hi when he got home.

Tom watched the old man step-step from the street to the yard, stopping by one of the kid's tricycles. It was on the edge of the street, tipped over. After standing next to the tricycle for a few moments, the old man eased over and with effort pulled it over to the porch. That tired him, and he stood still again, watching the three kids playing on the lawn. They didn't seem to notice he was there. He smiled as he watched their antics, but the smile was sad and distant.

Walking slowly to the blue spruce in the yard, he pinched some of the needles and held them up to his face. Tom knew how they smelled. Like New Hampshire, when his family was on vacation.

Most nights the old man went into the house after smelling the spruce needles. He started in that direction now, walking more slowly than usual. Then he stopped.

He stood turned away from Tom, and Tom looked where he looked, down the road, at the sunset. It got dark early now, and already the night air held the chill of the approaching winter. The old man took a step toward the sunset. The kids had gone inside. The cold air, the darkening sky, the sadness of the season—it turned the evening somber and hushed. Down the road, the sun went under, yellow changing to orange, to red, to crimson, to purple. The man step-stepped across the lawn and stooped to save a doll the little girl had left outside. He cradled it in his arms, heaved up the single step onto the porch, placed the doll carefully on the table there, and went inside.

When Tom woke, the sky was a cold gray. The kind of sky that brought snow. He peeked out, hoping to see snow on the ground. There was some! Not much, maybe a half inch. Not enough to cancel school. Too bad! Fall sure was over. It was as if Mother Nature had turned a switch. Last night, it had been fall. Now it was winter.

Across the street was a red fireman's truck. A small one, without ladders. The light was flick-flickering. Tom knew there was no fire. He hadn't heard any sirens. The truck wasn't a huge fire truck, just a small ambulance. Tom sensed something had happened to the old man.

The porch door opened, and two paramedics carried out a stretcher, the old man lying on it. They bumped the stretcher on the railing as they stepped down to the walkway. The old man flinched with pain. Other than that grimace, his face was lifeless, the color of a dead frog's belly. The woman held open the door, but she didn't walk to the ambulance. When the stretcher was out the door, she closed it. The old man was not dead. But his face was dead.

The two men pushed the stretcher into the ambulance. They started to close the doors, then one of them leaned in toward the old man. He straightened, spoke to the other paramedic who was climbing into the ambulance, then went over to the blue spruce. He broke off a sprig and carried it back to the ambulance, giving it to the old man before he closed the doors. A few moments later, the ambulance drove off.

Over the next few days, Tom noticed toys collecting on the lawn across the street. He began to make it a habit, after getting off the school bus, to pick up the wayward toys and put them on the porch. He felt good doing it; it made him think about the old man. He wondered if he was dead. But then, it didn't matter much. Living here or lying abandoned in a hospital or being dead, without love, it was all pretty much the same.

SURVIVAL

In the morning light, the last flares of the storm drifted thinly through the trees, through the pines and the spruce, to rest on heavy-laden boughs and sparkle on barren twigs. The snow undulated smoothly over rocks and logs, white where the rays of light touched, mauve and black and purple-brown under the darkness of the trees. It was a perfect morning—the surface of the snow unblemished, the heavens clearing, dawn sliding through the woods to add pastel colors to the drifts.

Beneath a toppled hemlock, a buck wakened. He was a big deer, not old but in his prime. He had weathered the autumn cold and the first part of the winter well; his coat had grown thick and a layer of fat had formed along his ribs. A few winters had taught him how and where to search for food. His bed was warm, and he woke slowly. He would not leave the shelter of the hemlock during the day; moving abroad in a new snow was dangerous. Not that the buck was aware that he would leave tracks. For him, it was enough to have been chased through snow in seasons past, enough to have been tracked in snow and to have been fired at. New snow meant danger, so he did not move except to test the breeze.

The last sparse flakes of the storm filtered through the pines as the buck listened and smelled. With the wind having died, the woods were quiet, as they are only when fresh powder soaks up all sound. The buck listened but there was nothing to hear, not the rustling in the leaves of a chipmunk, not the whispering of the wind in the trees. The woods were hushed. As dawn lightened, the woodland creatures gradually stirred. A chickadee scattered powder from a bush as it landed on a twig. Bits of falling pinecones attested to a red squirrel feeding high in a tree. And then the quiet was broken by a sharp noise, the hollow tap-tap-tapping of a woodpecker.

The buck lay with his head held high under the wind-fallen hemlock. He noticed the chickadee and the squirrel, heard the tapping of the woodpecker, but paid them no heed. He was fixed on the smell of a bobcat. For a long time, he sniffed the air, followed the scent as the bobcat searched upwind. Seeking smaller game, probably. An unwary squirrel or mouse, a grouse bedded under the snow, a careless snowshoe. As the buck smelled for the bobcat, the tapping of the woodpecker stopped. The buck turned his head to where the sound had been. Downwind.

He watched downwind, watched attentively. Downwind was dangerous; downwind movements made the buck nervous. For a long time, he watched and saw nothing. Then there was a sound, a scraping against bushes. The buck got to his feet. He did not want to leave his bed, did not want to forego the shelter of the wind-fallen hemlock. But the downwind sound made him nervous. He stood and watched.

The buck could not see the man who cursed as he brushed loose snow from his neck. The man did not curse hatefully, rather muttered good-naturedly at the snow that had sifted into the neck of his coat as he pushed through the thick bushes. The man liked the snow. Not down his neck perhaps, but he liked the clean of snow. Fresh, unblemished, it was perfect for tracking. He brushed the melting flakes from the nape of his neck and blew the light powder from the sights of his 30-30 before pushing on.

The man was a trapper. Jude, he was called, and he trapped because it was what he knew best. Jude was getting on, and each fall when he packed his winter supplies out of Salmonville, the storekeeper nodded good-bye and figured it would be the last time. But each spring, Jude showed up with a few furs, muskrat mostly, an occasional mink or red fox, and the hides of a couple of bobcats on which he collected bounty. Jude had been hunting the mountains around Salmonville for some fifty years, and he'd long been acknowledged the best hunter and trapper in the region. If he didn't make much money at hunting and trapping, it was only because he didn't want to. All he wanted was to shoot and trap enough so that he wouldn't go hungry. Some people in Salmonville said Jude didn't like to kill, but others laughed and asked, then why was he a hunter? And why did he live high up in the mountains? Only one or two people in Salmonville had ever seen Jude's cabin. There was no road to the cabin, not even a vague path. It was a good dozen hours of hiking from any sign of civilization. It was said Jude never returned twice to the cabin along the same route, that he did not want to sully the woods with a worn path. People smirked at his eccentricities, but no one questioned his skills as a mountain man.

The buck stood, hidden in the thick of the windfall, looking in the direction of the man. He knew something was coming, for again he heard bushes being thrust aside. Yet the buck did not move. There was no scent yet, and the deer did not know whether the movement meant danger or not. He didn't wish to leave the comfort of his bed until he was forced to. Then the buck saw the man. He watched for a while as Jude moved closer, watched calmly until it was clear the man was coming straight for the hemlock. Then the buck turned and slipped from the shelter of the downed tree. He trotted away for a hundred yards and looped downwind, looped until he was behind the man and could follow his scent. When he could smell the trapper, the buck stood in a thicket of small pines. He would wait until the trapper had passed far upwind. Then he would return to his bed.

Jude pushed through the snow toward a downed hemlock. He didn't move fast but he didn't stop much. He had been waiting for a new snow to go hunting, waiting for the deep winter cold that would keep a carcass frozen through the winter. Though he usually was able to shoot a snowshoe or a squirrel while running his trap line, he needed a side of venison. Without the guarantee of a side of venison frozen in his freezer box, a man had little chance to survive the winter. Jude didn't stop much this morning for there was no sense to it: no self-respecting deer would be moving today. He would have to jump one from its bed or chance across a set of tracks. Finding a set of tracks was just a matter of covering enough ground. When he found the tracks, then the hunt would begin.

When Jude passed the wind-fallen hemlock, he saw the buck's prints in the snow. He backtracked a few feet until he came to the bed. He felt the bed with his hands but could feel no warmth in the snow. It didn't surprise him. He'd never felt a snow-bed that was warm. He figured it wasn't warm even with the deer in it. He saw where the deer had stood, watching in the direction from where he had just come. Saw how the deer had turned to sneak away, not bounding in fear at the sight of the hunter as most deer would. From the tracks, Jude could see it was a big one. He shook his head slowly as he studied the tracks, memorizing their shape and size. Not just a big one, a really big one. Had to be a buck. And he'd been around a while. Ten years? Twelve?

The trapper sat on the toppled hemlock, his rifle across his knees, and fiddled in his pocket for the makings of a cigarette. Downwind, the buck still stood in the thicket of pines. He smelled the trapper, then smelled the bitterness of tobacco smoke. Jude smoked for five or ten minutes. While he smoked, he watched the trees all around, watched carefully. There was no hurry. If he didn't push the deer, the deer wouldn't run. And occasionally this was an easy way to shoot a careless deer—wait to see if he returned to his bed.

When Jude finished the cigarette, he took a last look around and then followed the tracks. He went right along, not hurriedly but persistently. The deer remained in the thicket of pines, smelled Jude moving away from the bed. The deer was not frightened. He was aware of the danger of the man, but he knew how to cope with danger. He had been hunted many times. The deer followed Jude's scent, followed as the trapper went upwind along the track, then looped just as the buck had. In a few minutes, he saw the man along his back trail. The buck moved then, trotted through the thicket of pines. Upwind. With the man behind him, he would not be able to return to his bed, yet he was reluctant to relinquish the shelter of the hemlock entirely. So, the deer did not run away from the bed, but looped back around it once more. He stopped downwind of the man, in the same pine thicket as before. He could smell the man as he tracked upwind and around.

Jude smiled when he saw that the deer had looped again. He could see from the tracks that the deer had not run, that he wasn't scared. The two downwind loops and the lack of fright told Jude this deer knew his stuff, that he had been hunted before. It was not going to be an easy hunt, and Jude would need to be patient. He again followed the tracks in the snow, followed toward where the buck waited in the pines. The two of them, the man and the buck, were now tied by the tracks, tied as firmly as if by an invisible rope. The deer would try to break away; the man would try to hang on to his end of the string of tracks.

When the buck saw the trapper on his back trail again, fear fluttered in him. He watched the man as he hiked through the snow, watched until the man was behind a thick spruce. Then he slipped through the stand of pines. Returning to the wind-fallen hemlock with the man behind was impossible. So the deer retraced the first part of the trail made by him and the man but did not turn back to make the loop. Instead, he continued almost straight into the wind.

Jude stopped as he neared the stand of pines. He searched the pines for a sign of the buck, searched in hope the buck would be unguarded and show himself. He saw where the tracks turned, saw where the buck had stood as he watched along his back trail. The buck had then loped between the shoulder-high pines in the same direction as before. Jude smiled when the tracks joined the other set, noticed where the deer's prints were on top of his own. He'd have to look more closely now to be sure he followed correctly, not that the tracking was hard. Before, there had been only one set of tracks; now there were two, old and new. He had only to be careful not to miss where the buck struck off the old trail.

So, Jude trailed behind, not moving fast but purposely. He scanned the trees ahead as he walked in hopes of glimpsing the deer. But he did not stop to look, for he was sure the deer would be cautious. Later in the day, perhaps, the deer might be careless. Or tomorrow. But not this early in the hunt.

After leaving the stand of pines, the buck trotted for a while before he stopped under a spruce to wait. He waited for a long time before he saw the man. The buck turned then and started upwind again. Jude found where the deer had stood under the spruce but did not pause. He pushed on along the track, following under the spruce with its branches burdened with snow, following between the straight trunks of the northern pines. It was quiet in the woods, and there seemed no life except for the deer and the man, their destinies bound by the tracks in the snow.

The deer continued trotting and waiting and trotting again. Behind him, Jude scuffed through the snow, noting always where the deer had stood in wait. It was a patient deer, he could see. The deer did not panic but simply kept ahead. This was going to be a long hunt.

Toward the middle of the afternoon, the buck changed direction but not his tactics. He waited in a thicket until the trapper appeared, then turned and trotted and waited again. Jude trudged behind, not changing his pace, though he did stop once to eat. From under his parka, he pulled out a rolled flapjack. Some would call it a sourdough pancake; Jude just called it a flapjack. Inside the flapjack was a bit of gravy and rabbit left over from the night before. He slapped the snow from a log with his hat and sat down. He ate the rolled flapjack, then started along the trail once more.

The deer pushed ahead when he saw the trapper again.

The buck wanted to lie down, so was heading for a stand of thick spruce clustered above even thicker juniper bushes. Instinct drove him to the shelter of the bushes. In the stand of spruce, the juniper was so thick that the buck had to leap to get through. After bounding and trotting through the juniper, he bedded down on a hillock where he could watch for the trapper.

The afternoon was wearing on when Jude reached the spruce and juniper bushes. Less than two hours of light, he figured. That meant an hour more of hunting and an hour to get home. He smiled wryly when he saw the buck had shoved through the junipers. It was the hardest tracking of all. He went more slowly now, standing long in one spot until he saw where the deer had gone. Tracking in junipers was hard because there was no smooth surface that showed the tracks. There were only up-thrusting bushes with snow scattered loosely over them. Jude had to stand where the buck had passed and scan ahead until he saw where snow had been brushed from the tips of the junipers. Then he would move a few feet. Often, he had to circle to pick up the tracks again. It was slow work. Most hunters would have lost patience and given up the chase. But Jude was not in a hurry. He was not hunting for sport, not hunting for fun. For him, as well as for the deer, it was a question of survival.

The buck lay for a long time before he saw the man. He was reluctant to get up, but the fear of the man was growing within him. Keeping low, he slipped from the hillock and trotted away from the man and out of the junipers. Trotted across the smooth surface of the snow between the trunks of the northern pines. Even here, in the comparative open between the black trunks, the daylight was fading.

Jude found where the deer had lain in the junipers. He did not pause but pushed on after the spoor. It was easier here, for the buck had run in a straight line. He followed through the junipers until he reached the open of the northern pines. Stopping, he could see the tracks ahead, like splotches of blood on the smooth snow, the darkness creeping like mist into the upper reaches of the northern pines. The trunks rose into the gloaming above, columns of a vast cathedral. The tracks would be easy to follow here. They seemed to pull at him with an invisible force, but Jude resisted. There was just light enough to reach camp. Reluctantly he turned and headed back to the cabin.

The buck stood for a long time as the darkness filled the hollows under the northern pines. Even after the last light faded and night had settled, the buck waited for the man. It was much later when he pawed under an apple tree for the frozen, thawed, and refrozen fruit; pawed in the snow for the apples soured bittersweet by the sun and frost. And it was later still when the buck lay sleeping in dry leaves in a thicket of scrub oak. He slept deeply, resigned it seemed to the inevitable pursuit by the hunter.

With the first light, the buck awakened to listen and smell. The day was cold and the air thin, the dead leaves of the scrub oak frozen, unmoving. The buck dozed and listened, dozed and listened as daylight crept under the trees. Later in the morning, he started into wakefulness. The odor of the trapper was in the air. The buck waited until the smell was clear to him. As the odor gained strength, he heard the man. The buck slipped from the thicket of scrub oak, bounded through a stand of spruce, settled into a trot. When he could no longer smell the man, he turned behind a broken pine stump to watch his back trail.

Jude had awoken when the stars were still steely sparks in the sky. After stoking his potbellied stove, he brewed two cups of coffee over it and poured flour and water mixed with a bit of sourdough into a skillet. As he ate a flapjack and drank the coffee, the stars faded outside. He rolled another flapjack into a pocket of his parka. The flapjack was dry for he had finished the last of the rabbit the night before. It was cold in the cabin, but Jude warmed himself near the stove before he shrugged on the parka. He drank the second cup of coffee standing in the doorway. The light was coming, and he could make out the edges of the clearing around his cabin, could see the darkness that was the woodpile. The sky looked clear, and he hoped the weather would hold. A new snow would cover the deer's tracks.

When it was light enough, he shoved four cartridges into the 30-30, some extras into a pocket, and started out of the clearing. He backtracked his footsteps from the night before to where he had left the deer's trail. He turned then and took to the trail once more.

Jude followed the tracks through the pines to where the buck had stood so long, followed through the woods to where he had fed. Rather than try to work out the trail where the deer had pawed and scratched for apples, he circled around the tracks until he found where the buck had struck off once more. The trapper walked steadily along the tracks. The sooner he jumped the deer, the sooner he would get a shot. Today, he figured, the deer would get careless. With luck, he would get a shot by afternoon. He hoped it wouldn't snow before then.

He walked through the northern pines to a section where the big trees had been lumbered. Piles of slash, rotted out, formed mounds under the snow; and gray birch had sprouted where the trees had been felled. Scrub oak grew thick, and he had to shove through the tangle that scratched at his parka.

He stopped. He had heard something. Squatting to peer under thc scrub, he waited for a few minutes, then pushed on. He thought he had jumped a deer. A few yards farther, he found the bed where the buck had lain. Beyond the bed, light, scattered powder marked where the buck had bounded, and three or four feet farther along, new prints. The trail was fresh again.

The buck waited behind the broken pine stump, waited anxiously to discover whether the man was on his trail. The air smelled cold with no hint of danger, just the scent of the pine woods and the musty odor of a nearby porcupine den. Then, after a long wait, the danger, the scent of the man, was in the air. The buck saw the man and left the pine stump. He circled around the trapper and headed back to the cover of the scrub oak. He followed his own trail backward through the scrub oak, branching off before reaching his bed. He turned in the cover to wait. The deer had followed his own tracks backward many times when being trailed. It was not his to understand why he did this; but in the past it had led to losing his tracker, had confused a less experienced hunter, a hunter unable to work out the intricacies of multiple, jumbled marks in the snow.

Jude followed the deer. With no trouble, he found the spot where the buck had waited behind the pine stump, found where the deer had circled back to hide his own trail in the scrub oak. Jude shook his head when the old and new trails joined in the brush, the weathered wrinkles on his face pulling into a half smile of admiration. Again, he thought, this was no yearling but an experienced buck. He almost hoped the deer would outsmart him; even considered breaking off the trail. But after a few minutes of scanning ahead and to both sides, he continued his tracking. He had no choice. Winter would soon descend in fury, and he needed the venison to survive her wrath and cold. Almost reluctantly, he continued on.

The deer waited for the man. He heard the crashing in the bushes for a long time before the noise came too close. Then he slipped away, loping into the pines and along a ridge. He did not go far before turning to wait.

Jude forced his way out of the thicket of scrub oak into the easier going under the trees. He followed the deer through the pines as before, the deer trotting ahead, waiting, and then slipping away as Jude neared. The deer did not stay far ahead, and Jude noticed this, knew well the buck was tiring. He figured he'd get a shot before noon. Only a few minutes later, he caught a glimpse of the deer for the first time. It was a buck all right, as Jude had figured. He was a magnificent creature; Jude had rarely seen a more handsome animal. Again, he almost quit the trail, but the line of prints pulled him forward inexorably, as if the two of them, hunter and hunted, were bound by a chain.

The tracking in the pine woods was easy, for the spoor showed plainly on the smooth snow between the trunks. Jude didn't watch the tracks much now but scanned ahead. It was time for the buck to get negligent, time for a shot. Often it took a day for Jude to get a deer, occasionally two days, but almost always he had gutted the kill before the second afternoon.

The buck stayed ahead of the man, leading him through the pine woods. Fear was rising in the buck, a blind thrashing inside him. He had been hunted before, had been hunted often, but never had the danger been there so long, so tenaciously. Always the men had followed, always the deer had stayed ahead. That had been enough. After a few hours, the men were no longer there. But now the danger did not vanish, it persisted.

The buck bounded partway up a hillside to where a trail, a deer trail, followed the contour below the ridge. He turned onto the trail, ran along it, and stopped by a spruce to wait for the man. He could see the trapper far off between the trunks of the pines, could see him reach the hillside and stop. For a long time, the buck watched as the man stood looking. Then the man started up the hill. The buck turned and continued along the deer trail, and then angled off to climb the ridge and wait again at the top.

Jude followed the buck up the hillside, to where the animal had turned onto the deer trail. The snow was marked with a slew of confused tracks coming and going. He studied them until he was convinced he could recognize the prints of his buck among the others. It was not all that difficult, for the buck's prints were the largest of the lot.

A smaller deer would have eluded a hunter here, its tracks lost in the blur of impressions in the snow. More slowly now, Jude scuffed along the deer trail, pausing every time a deer had branched uphill or down, pausing to scrutinize the imprint and decide whether it had been his buck.

Above, at the top of the ridge, the buck stood screened behind a small pine, watching the trapper as he advanced along the contour of the hill below. This brought the danger closer for a while, until the man was directly downhill from the deer, and then the danger receded as the man passed below and continued farther along the deer trail. Jude had missed the spot where the buck had left the deer trail and headed straight up the hillside.

The buck watched as the man appeared and disappeared among the trees, watched as he plodded farther and farther away. After a while, he saw the man pause for a few minutes, then pivot and start back. Directly below the deer, the trapper turned again, this time climbing toward the top of the ridge. The danger had returned.

The buck left the small pine, trotted over the ridge, and down the other side. Until now the buck had been working mostly into the wind. Working into the wind was safe. There were never any surprises. The breeze drifting toward the deer alerted him to any danger long before he stumbled upon it. But the buck was tiring, he wanted to lie down. He left the safety of the breeze and turned downhill, turned to where he knew there was heavy cover, cover where he could hide. And rest.

On reaching the crest of the ridge, Jude slapped snow off a log with his hat and sat. He was tired from the climbing. He had lost the buck's track in the jumble of the deer trail on the hillside. Such a hodgepodge of tracks had to be comforting to the deer, for by joining them he'd probably thrown previous hunters off his trail. Indeed, Jude had lost the trail himself, but had realized it and backtracked to where the deer had left the trail and started uphill.

Jude reached for the flapjack inside his parka. He was tired and had no appetite, but he forced himself to chew and swallow. Much as he wanted to break off the hunt, he had no choice. If the weather turned and snowed him in before he could pack in a side of venison… He did not finish the thought. As he sat, he scanned the hillside below. The line of the buck's trail was clear. He could trace it for a goodly distance from his perch as it led down and to his left through the open forest. That direction, as he knew all too well, descended toward the river and the swamp around it. The buck had left the safety of moving upwind and was seeking the safety of heavy cover and darkness of the swamp. Walking and trailing in the muck and dense alder there would be difficult and tiring. Damned smart deer, Jude thought. He hoped he got a good shot before the buck reached the swamp.

Jude trailed on, stopping often to scan the shapes and shadows ahead. The deer could not be far, since every two hundred yards, Jude saw where the tracks turned—where the buck had stood in wait. On the first day, the buck had stopped every half mile or so. Now he didn't go as far. Like Jude, the buck was tiring. Physically perhaps, and more certainly tiring mentally. Under the trees, the afternoon light was dimming. Spotting the deer would not be easy. About another hour, Jude figured, and he would have to start for the cabin.

The buck kept making for the swamp with the man behind. The fear was still in the deer, but it was a dull fear, dull because he was tired. The fear kept him ahead of the trapper, but the distance diminished. Instinct drove the deer to the swamp, to the closeness of the alders and the darkness. When he neared the swamp, he turned in a clump of hazelnuts to watch for the man.

It was a long time before he saw him. The trapper pushed under a spruce, and the buck could plainly see the white of his face, he was that close. Fear exploded in the buck, and his sinews convulsed as he leapt from the thicket. Jude jerked the gun to his shoulder but did not shoot wild through the brush. There was no sense in it; he didn't have a clear shot.

The buck ran toward the swamp, and for a long time Jude could hear the crashing of the bushes. The buck had been plenty scared. Following through the swamp, judging from the clatter of the deer's passage, would be hard work.

With the light fading, Jude pushed on into the swamp. The walking was arduous with the alders closely knit, but the buck's panicked trail, gouged and gashed into the snow, was easy to follow. He followed until the buck had jumped a brook. Then he turned and, with the night fast coming, headed for the cabin.

After running through the alders, the deer trotted more slowly, his fear subsiding. He turned finally and waited as the darkness swallowed the swamp around him. He waited for the trapper, waited for a long time, but the danger did not come. Finally, the buck chewed at the tips of the alders near him. He browsed half-heartedly, for he was weary. It was not long before he bedded under two spruces, which formed an island amongst the alders and the water and muck of the swamp.

With the first light, Jude latched the cabin door and followed his footsteps of the night before. He followed to where he had left the deer's trail at the brook and struck off after the buck. Today he would get a shot, Jude knew. Yesterday he had sighted the buck twice; today the deer would be more tired and hence careless. Rarely had a deer stayed ahead of him for more than a day and a half, and he could not recall having tracked one for more than two days. The buck was unlucky, Jude thought. The weather had held cold, but it hadn't snowed. An inch or two of new snow and the hunt would have been over. Jude sighed. His own good fortune was the buck's bad luck.

Under the spruce, the deer waited for the man, alert for the breaking of twigs or the cracking of ice. At the first sound, he was on his feet, smelling for the danger. But it was not the man, merely a fox heading for his den and breaking through the crisp crust of ice that formed where frozen water met mud. Although the sound had been a fox, the buck stood for a long time listening. Then he heard the man coming again. The deer fled from the two spruces into the thickness of the alders, where he waited for the danger.

Jude found the bed under the two spruces and followed the tracks from the spruce into the alders. The going was difficult and he was tired, but he went cautiously, looking always ahead. Given the frozen swamp crackling underfoot and the dense brush scraping his jacket, it seemed to him he was as loud as a crazed, galloping moose. He slowed his pace, forced himself into silence. As he peered ahead, he shouldered his rifle from time to time to sight on a distant object, testing lines of vision. Shooting in the alders would be well-nigh impossible. A bullet wouldn't travel far through the brush.

The buck listened for the movements of the man. He could not see far but heard the man as he shoved between entwined branches. The deer slipped away, waited until he heard the man again, slipped away again. He turned and twisted and looped in the alders, yet always when he stopped, the danger was behind. The tracks in the snow tied the man and the deer; there was no way to cut that bond.

Jude sweated from the heavy going in the swamp. The deer was never far ahead, he had even spotted him twice, yet he couldn't get a good shot. He followed ever more slowly, watching, watching, looking for a shape or movement. Through the undergrowth, he saw the deer again. Moving his head, Jude tried to find an opening for a shot.

The buck leaped at the thunder as wood splinters showered and hit him. Through the alder swamp he thrashed, bushes crashing at his charge, until he burst into the open under some beeches. For a long time, he sprinted, dodging trees and jumping logs, running blindly from the gun until his trembling legs could run no more.

The deer stood for a long time under the sweeping branches of a beech, his legs quivering, his head hanging in fatigue, not listening, not smelling. As his legs shook less violently, he finally watched and smelled again. It was a long time before the man came into view. The buck watched the man slip down the slope under the beeches, watched as he came nearer. The fear rose in the buck, but it rose slowly, not so great as before. Yet the buck turned, the fear forcing him into a sluggish trot.

It was noon when the man found where the deer had stood under the beech. It had run the better part of a mile, he figured. Maybe more than that. It was a long way for a deer to run. Jude followed the trail, noticed that the hoof prints were closer together now, noticed the troughs in the snow connecting them. The deer's strides were shorter, and he was dragging his hooves. Jude looked ahead, watched for movement between the silver-gray trunks, certain the buck would show himself.

The deer saw the man once more and turned from behind a beech. As he turned, Jude saw him and fired at the spot above the foreleg. The deer heard the thunder, lost his balance as he jumped, and smashed into a tree with his shoulder. The buck ran, and as he ran a storm lashed the trees in fury and a thousand bees whirled inside him. The bees stung, and then the roaring storm was not a storm but the rasping of his breath, which softened to a bubbling like the gurgle and the frothing of a trout stream as it pitched out of the stillness of a pool and down a rocky shallow run.

Jude walked to where he had shot the buck. Patches of blood splattered over the snow. The deer had run but would not go far. He levered the empty cartridge from the rifle and pushed another one in. He leaned the 30-30 against the silver of a beech, fumbled for papers and tobacco in his pocket. Slowly, Jude rolled a cigarette as he looked at the bright, frothy red bubbles on the snow.

A lung shot. The deer would not go far. He would lie down, and if he wasn't pushed, his lungs would fill with blood and the wound would stiffen until he couldn't rise. It was better to wait and let nature run its course than to chase hard, driving the deer to run once more. Jude was tired from the chase. He always felt tired at the end, even when the hunt had been short. Must be the concentration, he figured. It had been a beautiful buck, and he had hit him squarely.

Jude finished the cigarette, rolled another. A few minutes later, he rolled yet one more. He was in no hurry. The end of a hunt was always anticlimactic, drained him of energy. He watched the smoke of his cigarette rise in the still air, listened wanly as a red squirrel on a nearby branch scolded him. When his mind had quieted, he stubbed out the cigarette, reluctantly stood up. He now had to finish the job. Cradling the 30-30, he followed the bright red splotches in the snow, followed the trail of blood that led him to the kill.

The buck was down behind a tree, unable to rise. Jude pulled his hunting knife and carefully slit the deer's throat. Convulsions shook the animal, and slowly the eyes dimmed as the blood drained from him. Jude stood for a minute, counting the points on the buck's rack, noting where the bullet had entered. He shook his head in admiration of the creature's size and weight. A sadness, an emptiness, welled within him. He spat against the beech before slitting the deer's belly to gut it. With one arm, he reached into the cavity to spill the entrails onto the snow, where they formed a steaming heap. He reached inside again, deeper inside the cavity, and tugged and tore to loosen the heap from its attachments. Again, he thought that the buck had been a handsome creature. Jude looked up from the entrails and gazed for a moment at the forest he loved, then shook his head ever so slightly.

Returning to his work, he cleaned blood from the cavity with handfuls of snow, then wiped the worst of the blood from his hands and arm. Carefully, he folded the heart and liver into the bit of oilskin in which he had wrapped his flapjack, stuffed it into the game pocket of his coat. With his knife and the piece of rope he used as a belt, he fashioned a crude travois from two saplings and tied the buck between them. Pulling the burden, he started for home.

The buck was heavy, and Jude was sweating hard long before he reached his cabin. Under the open beeches, the travois had been a good idea, but as Jude reached the foot of the knoll on which his cabin stood, the travois became entangled in the brush and thorns that grew there. He untied the deer from the poles, fastened one end of the piece of rope to the buck's rack, laid the other end over his shoulder, and knotted it around his waist. Thus fastened, he leaned into the rope and pulled the deer up the hill. He was exhausted by the time he reached the clearing. Still tied to the buck, he stood, not moving, breathing heavily.

As daylight faded, it started to snow. It was no more than a flurry, but a harbinger of what the night might bring. He brushed the fresh snow from his jacket and returned to the task at hand. He freed himself from the cord binding him to the deer and kneeled next to its head. Inserting his hunting knife under the buck's chin, he cut a slit between the two sides of the jawbone, into the deer's mouth. He forced the rope into the slit from the outside of the jawbone and into the mouth, just below the tongue. Pulling the cord out of the mouth, he knotted the two ends together to create a loop. Years ago, on the white oak next to his woodpile, he had hung a rope with a hook on the end from a pulley on an overhanging branch. Dozens of deer had hung from the hook over the years.

He dragged the buck to the spot below the hook, lowered it to the ground, and looped the cord attached to the deer's jawbone over the hook. In this way he avoided needing to lift the deer at all. Pulling the free end of the rope raised the deer's head off the ground, and then the whole of the buck was aloft. He stopped pulling when the hind legs were still lightly touching the ground. That kept the carcass from swinging and turning while he did the skinning. He tied the free end of the rope to the trunk of the oak. With fistfuls of snow, he wiped the interior of the carcass once again until it was free of blood, improving on the field dressing of two hours before. Blood would turn the meat black, even cause spoilage when the meat was frozen.

From his pocket, Jude pulled a jackknife. The blade was hardly two inches in length, thin as a razor, honed to an edge far sharper than his hunting knife. He spent a few minutes trimming inside the cavity, snipping off loose bits of meat, of diaphragm, of spots where the organs had been attached. Then he caught the skin of the carcass just below the breastbone, slipped the jackknife under the skin, and slit the deer's hide along the chest and the neck to within a few inches of the lower jawbone. Next, he turned the blade and continued the slit as if he were tracing a necklace around the buck's head, keeping to just behind the ears. Once the head had been circled, he moved to each of the forelegs. Again, he cut a slit, this time across the chest to the armpit and up the inner side of the foreleg to within a few inches of the hoof, then encircled the leg. He cut similar slits along the second foreleg and then the hind legs.

Finished with the cutting, he grasped the hide at the cut near the ears. With his fingers and the jackknife, he loosened a flap of skin. When he had loosed enough to allow a firm grasp, he pulled downward, peeling the hide from the carcass. The more hide he peeled, the easier the process became. Once or twice, he used the jackknife to free the skin at stubborn spots, mostly where the legs met the torso. When the detached hide reached the tailbone, he cut through it with his hunting knife, and then pulled once more to release the last of the hide from the carcass. With the hide completely off, he rubbed the naked carcass clean with handfuls of snow.

Pausing to inspect his work, he rubbed a few more spots with snow, admired the thick white slabs of subcutaneous fat on the buck's sides and rump. The buck had eaten well in preparation for the winter. Nature had been good to him, had provided a bountiful supply of autumn mast.

Jude loosened the rope from the tree trunk and hoisted the carcass so that the rear hocks were eight feet off the ground. Bears might be hibernating, but coyotes, cougars, wolverines, and bobcats were all hungry in the winter. Once the meat was frozen hard, he would butcher it into quarters and transfer it to his snow box. The box stood along the north side of the cabin and was fitted with a stout, tight-fitting lid. After he put the meat in the box, he would pack snow around it, filling the box completely.

As darkness gathered under the trees, Jude carried a couple armloads of firewood from the woodpile to the cabin's porch, and one armload inside the cabin to the small stack next to the potbellied stove. Before shedding his boots, he filled his snow pot and placed it on the stove to melt the snow. He restarted the dying embers in the firebox, dropped some deer fat into a skillet, added a few dried wild mushrooms and onions he had collected during the summer. While the onions browned, he sliced the buck's liver. The skillet simmered as the gloaming crept between the trees. Jude cooked the liver slowly to keep it tender, diced an apple he had rescued from a long-gone orchard, and added it to the pan a few minutes before the cooking was done.

He ate slowly, savoring the food, sipping ice-cold water from the snow pot. He was hungry. It was his first real meal in the three days since the hunt began. As he ate, night settled around the cabin. Stars twinkled beyond the bare branches of the oaks. It would be a cold night. Even in the cabin, Jude could feel the temperature drop. He pulled the cabin's one chair near the stove, took out his whetstone, and absentmindedly stropped his jackknife.

Later, he went to the door of the cabin to look at the night before going to sleep. From the porch he could see the dark patch that was the woodpile and the shape of the buck where it hung. He stood, unmoving, looking upward into the darkness as if in a spell. As he watched, the sky thickened, obscuring the stars. The weather had changed. Jude stirred, inhaled deeply. Snow. The smell of snow in the air. A shiver ran along the nape of his neck. It would be coming down in bushels before morning. There had already been two or three small snows in the past weeks. This would be the first real one, a three- or four-day blizzard. Old Man Winter in full fury. Drifts would soon be waist deep, perhaps up to his chin. He had lucked out. Shoot a deer too early, the carcass would spoil before the winter freeze hit; shoot it after the snow lay deep, dragging the carcass to the cabin became a monumental, perhaps impossible, task.

With the smell of the coming snow in the air, he put off heading to his bunk, but ferried instead armloads of wood from the woodpile to the porch. It would save him struggling through deep drifts in the morning. When the porch was packed, he closed the door, pulled in the latch string, banked the fire, and headed for his bunk. He smiled to himself as the wind picked up and tree branches rattled. Let Old Man Winter roar. With food in the larder, he would be there to greet Mistress Spring when she began her dance.

SWEET DEBORAH

The cab swung up to the curb. He climbed in, gave the cabbie Deborah's address, and eased back into the cushions, enjoying the pleasant feeling of well-being. He had just left the Coq-au-Vin where he dined two or three times every week, and the Chateauneuf and the duck simmered in orange sauce still glowed warmly within him. Life was good. A whiskey sour and checking his mail and scrolling through the news while they prepared his meal, dinner with wine followed by cheese, coffee, and cognac. Not too bad. Comfortable. Luxurious even.

Yes, he liked his life. He had graduated eight, no, nine years ago from Harvard Law, got a job as an associate at the firm right away, thanks to Senator Schumer and good ole Dad. He had started at one hundred sixty and gotten cost-of-living increases since. It didn't make him rich, he had to watch what he spent, but even in New York he could squeeze out a small apartment that he'd had professionally decorated, good food, plenty of Johnny Walker, and … Well, what else was there? Cable, smartphone, dues at the tennis club, and a couple of dates each week with Deborah. He didn't need a car. As long as he stayed away from the wife-and-kids trap, he had it made. Keep his head down, stay below the radar. He'd be damned if he would work his ass off trying to become a partner at the firm. He liked things just as they were.

Except for Deborah, he thought, and his forehead wrinkled in perplexity. What was he going to do about that sweet creature? She was becoming dependent on him, fond of him, was allowing their relationship to become a major portion of her life. And it wasn't just her. He too was becoming emotionally entangled. It was what always happened. All he desired was a simple, straightforward relationship that satisfied those two cursed human needs: companionship and sex. So simple, but it never seemed to work. The woman always got emotionally involved, and then he did, and the relationship metastasized, threatening them both. So, he would have to end it with Deborah—but he was a coward. He'd known months ago he'd have to walk away, yet he kept putting it off. The last thing he wanted was to hurt Deborah, and breaking up with her would certainly hurt her. Yet it had to be done. The breakup would hurt them both, but the pain would be short-term. The longer he waited, the worse it would be.

He crushed the unpleasant thought as if he were crushing a cigarette butt and glanced out the window. The taxi sped through Central Park, a black void between the brilliance of the East and West Sides, whose tiered lights formed a mosaic of sparkling crystals set in a background of azures and violets and blacks. It was a damned fine city, he thought. Let the Boy Scouts have their star-studded skies and the hunters their purple mountain majesties. He preferred the bright lights of the city and the New York skyline. After all, it was easier to admire beauty from the Grand Havana Room with a brandy snifter in hand than it was when shivering in a tent coated with hoar frost; easier to appreciate Central Park from a taxi than the Rockies when stumbling up some rock-strewn arroyo, numb with fatigue. New York made living bearable … if one knew how to avoid its more unpleasant sides. For he was a realist and recognized that the city had unsavory aspects, but they could be avoided if one knew the rules. Don't go too far uptown, don't get ambitious and muscle with your colleagues for a better position on the corporate ladder, don't go to Coney Island in good weather. Keep to the relaxed atmosphere of good restaurants and nightclubs, be satisfied with a position that entails neither onerous responsibility nor work, avoid the common crowd. He smiled at his axioms, recalling that there was one more: don't cause anyone pain. Which brought him back to Deborah.

He wished to hell she'd heeded his advice. When had he warned her? Nearly two years ago now, shortly after they started dating. They'd gone out to eat. Not to the Coq-au-Vin, naturally, for that was his private sphere that he did not want spoiled at some later time by intrusive memories. Probably Chez Martin or the Near East. Not that it mattered. All that was important was that he had warned her; but she, of course, had not heeded the advice. Nor had he, and he guessed he couldn't blame either of them. Bedroom intimacy just made detachment impossible. One either became disgusted with oneself and ended the affair, or one grew emotionally attached, rather like a barnacle anchoring itself to a rock. There seemed to be no middle road.

What had he said to her? He tried to recall. Yes, now he remembered. They had been at the Near East. But it hadn't been when they first met. It was about six months later, just after they began sleeping together.

"Look, Deborah," he had said, "we ought to get a few things straight before either of us gets burned." He had smiled across the table at her, a bit embarrassed. “We’ve got to think about where we’re headed … what we’re doing.”

She had nodded in agreement, so he continued.

“We’ve known each other how long? Six months now?” Again, she nodded. “Ever since we met, I’ve been thinking about us. We get along well, damned well even, but I often wonder why. You adore kids, I don’t. You like the country, I don’t.” He shrugged, not able to think of any significant differences in their personalities. The subject was difficult to discuss, and she wasn’t helping him, remaining silent, watching him closely.

He forged on. “I guess what I’m trying to say is that although we like each other, we can’t expect too much. I don’t see much in the future for us. I don’t think …” He spread his hands wide, palms upward, futilely searching for the words that would tactfully convey his meaning.

“You mean you don’t think we should get married?” she asked.

“Well, yes. No, not exactly,” he added, hedging, not wanting to hurt her, but then he came clean. “Yes. I can’t quite see us being compatible in ten or twelve years. Even though we get along fine right now.” He paused, somewhat fearful of the effect of his words, but then pushed on. “You’re at the age when a woman begins dreaming of marriage, so I thought it only fair that you should know how I feel.”

She smiled, a bit sadly, he thought, but bravely agreed with him. “I want to marry, Tim, but I’m in no hurry. I’ve always believed a woman should work for a few years before she settles down. It increases her perspective. So, don’t feel embarrassed if our relationship is only temporary. It’s just what I want.”

"Good," he replied, though he realized she didn't mean what she had said, even though she probably believed it herself. "Good. It's just that, well, a woman can get awfully emotionally attached and … I don't want you to get hurt …" He trailed off lamely, not knowing what he could add to the warning, so he touched her hand where it lay on the table and ended the conversation.

That had been about a year ago, maybe more. Since then, they had seen each other three or four times a week, and they made love almost every time. They satisfied each other's needs quite well—except that Deborah didn't feel completely at ease when naked, and hence he didn't either, and this occasionally caused their lovemaking to be awkward. But on the whole, she was a satisfactory lover. And that, of course, was another reason he hated to break off with her. For she did satisfy him, and losing her would grieve him. Without her, his nights would be empty. They would be filled again eventually, but the interim would be painful. That was not really important, though. What was important was that they had allowed their lives to become too narrow. Neither of them had the time or desire to date anyone else. In addition, she was shy. It wasn't easy for her to make new friends. So, they had come to rely completely on each other for companionship—and sex. If they broke up, it would certainly upend their lives. Bad for him. Worse, he feared, for her. He hated to hurt her.

The taxi had left the park, and the driver stopped at a red light. A stiff winter wind buffeted the pedestrians on the sidewalk, and the cold had turned their faces various hues of crimson and blue. Hands stuffed deep in their pockets, they hurried to their destinations as gusts tugged and flapped around them. Tim shivered in empathy, damned glad he was in the cab, insulated and out of the wind. The pedestrians reminded him of Boy Scouts and hunters. Shivering, miserable. They didn't know enough to come in out of the cold.

He thought contentedly of Deborah's apartment. There, at least, it would be warm and bright. The cold wind would be part of another world. He'd fix a couple of drinks—maybe mulled wine would be good tonight—which they'd savor while listening to some good music. He felt in the mood for Tchaikovsky. *The Nutcracker,* possibly. Yes, *The Nutcracker*. He smiled as he compared the grace of the Sugar Plum Fairy, who danced in his mind as he hummed her song, with the lumpy form of the homeless woman hunched in the cold on the sidewalk. Yes, he was happy he was out of the wind, happy he'd soon be at Deborah's and wouldn't have to go out again until morning.

He cast about in his memories, recalling past winter evenings they had spent together at her condo, and laughed out loud when he remembered her last birthday. He'd had a caterer deliver dinner. What was it? Roast duckling? No, pheasant. And of course, he'd brought champagne. A couple of bottles. It had been a glorious dinner, and one of the few times he'd seen Deborah high. It must have been the champagne. She began dancing for him after the caterer left. She had been hilarious at first, a comic imitation of a striptease artist, then her style changed, and she was graceful and enticing. She danced to seduce him—and she had been marvelous. That night, she had not been embarrassed at being naked. As she danced, she stripped, and the less dressed she was, the more provocative her dancing became. They had made love wildly, and afterwards she admitted she had not understood him when they had first known each other.

"You never touched me," she told him. "For six months, you didn't so much as kiss me. It drove me wild."

"Not because I didn't want to," he replied.

"I knew that. That's what I couldn't understand. I wanted you, you wanted me. I started to look for someone else to satisfy myself… since I was sure that must be what you were doing."

He'd been surprised at her revelation, for she was not sexually adventurous. But it wasn't that revelation that made the evening memorable. It was the dance. He smiled. That had been quite a dance. It had even embarrassed him some, it had been that good.

The cab halted, and the driver hollered that this was the place. He paid and climbed out. Waiting at the foyer door for Deborah to buzz him in, he experienced a pang of guilt. He was letting her love him, and soon he'd be hurting her terribly. Right then he promised: he wouldn't desert her before Christmas. He'd make her holidays happy.

He took the elevator up and she was waiting, sparkling, at the far end of the carpeted hall. It always surprised him how mature she looked when he first caught sight of her, given how vulnerable he knew she was.

"You must be freezing," she called. "The weather's frightful."

She tilted her face up for a kiss as he reached her. "It is frightful," he agreed. "I took a taxi. You know me, never go out outside if it can be helped!"

"I know," she said with a laugh, drawing him into the apartment and closing the door. "How about fixing us a drink? I've been waiting hours."

She agreed to the mulled wine, so he puttered in the kitchen fixing it. When it was ready, he slipped a stick of cinnamon into each glass, poured in the aromatic brew, and joined her in the living room. The wine was delicious, and they savored its warmth as they chatted about this and that, catching up on gossip. Deborah didn't seem in the least sad, just as gay and vivacious as always.

In the cab going home, less than an hour later, Tim shook his head as he thought of her behavior. That was what he couldn't understand. As a matter of fact, he couldn't understand any of it. He tried to reconstruct the scene exactly as it had happened. They were sipping the wine and talking, and perhaps he had let his mind wander. And then, when he tuned in again, Deborah was recalling that they had both decided at the start that their relationship would be temporary. Then what had she said?

The taxi swayed around a corner, and he grabbed the door rest to steady himself. How had she put it?

"Remember that last year I said I wasn't ready for marriage? That I felt I could use some perspective?"

He had nodded, and she went on to say that now she felt ready. He had gulped, knowing she was going to suggest they get married. Panic rising, he waited for the proposal, wondering how he would tell her, without devastating her, that marriage was out of the question. But then she was saying, "… we've been going together for a couple of months. We've decided to move to Denver. He's got a great job offer out there."

He looked at her, stupefied, sure he'd misunderstood. She loves me. I know she loves me. How could she happily be telling him that she was moving to Denver with another guy? That she was planning to marry him?

He stared out the cab window. On the sidewalk, a few papers whirled in the gutter. Hardly anyone was out now in the cold wind. The taxi veered and headed through Central Park.

What else had she said? What did it mean? Pondering, playing the evening back in his mind, he realized her cheerfulness when he first arrived had been forced. She had been covering up. She hadn't been able to bear it any longer. She'd let herself love him too much. That other guy? That was just a story, a lure she threw out there to see if he would protest, ask her to marry *him*. He hadn't taken the bait. So, Denver was her excuse, her way out.

Damn, he thought. He had promised not to hurt her.

He glanced out the window and shivered. The trees in the park bent and swayed as the gale tore at them, leaves hurtling along the ground. A dog slunk forlorn and chilled past a bench. God! he thought. Am I ever glad I'm not out there! He suddenly had the weird premonition that he'd narrowly missed having to spend the night out in that cold. A shiver ran along his spine, and he leaned forward and asked the driver to turn up the heat.

Poor Deborah, he thought. She was a sweet kid. He hoped she'd be able to get her feet under her and get along without him. He was angry at himself for hurting her, and he knew the next few months would be hard for her, but she'd get over it. The thought she'd find someone else in a year or two consoled him. He shifted on the seat, trying to stop his shivering. As the air in the cab warmed, he stared out the window into the darkness that was the park. God knows, he thought, there was no way he was going into the cold out there.

THE GREAT NORTH WOODS

The fire was dying. He picked up the few remaining half-burned twigs and placed them over the fading embers, careful not to burn his fingers.

The bits of driftwood he had collected and not used he threw into the woods, each piece in a different direction. When the rocks were cleared of the unused debris, he returned his attention to the fire. He pushed dying embers and ashes together, coaxing them into a tongue of flame, wanting to burn them away in order to leave no sign of his passing.

He looked up, surveyed the lake. From where he squatted near the tip of the peninsula, he could see a great deal of its five-mile length, but given the lake's shape, three long arms joining in the middle, he couldn't see it all. He scanned across the water for any sign of life. He had been watching a half dozen loons feeding. They had moved a few hundred yards. It took a minute or two to spot them again. They spent more time underwater than on the surface. Any boats? He hadn't seen any yesterday or this morning. At first, he thought there were none. That pleased him. A wink of light off to the southeast caught his eye. A reflection. Off what? He squinted. The far shore was a mile or so away. Hard to make out anything at that distance. Again a wink of light. He tried to focus. There. Low on the water, all but invisible against the shoreline. Dark green, perhaps black. Most visible was the lump at one end. A canoe with a single paddler. Trolling a fly, probably. As he had been doing. But for the flash of sunlight on wet paddle, he wouldn't have spotted him.

He'd started fishing just before dawn. He'd been at it for a couple of hours. No hits. Hungry, he had paddled in to make a fire. He had beached the canoe on the tumble of naked rocks between the tangle of bushes and the water. After Labor Day, the dam here on Nesowadnehunk was lowered a foot. A week later, a canoe-length of rocks lined the shore below the summer waterline. Granite. Boulders and stones. Hunks of the Canadian Shield. He had arranged four flat rocks into a makeshift fireplace right on the edge of the water. The largest rock he had laid flat-side up; on that he had built the fire. The other three rocks he had set on edge, one left, one right, and one at the back. They would reflect the heat; more importantly, they hid the flames from anyone on the lake. He had built a teepee of twigs on the flat rock, had placed a roll of dry birch bark under the teepee and lit it. As the birch bark and then the twigs flared, he had fed the blaze with sticks no thicker than his thumb, all shorter than the blade of his sheaf knife. He wanted just enough fire to toast a slice of bread. He had no wish to wait all morning for a large cook fire to blaze, burn, and then die.

With his knife he had cut a small branch from a shrub, twelve inches or so below where two twigs branched out, forming a V. He pulled off the leaves, placed a slice of bread on the spread of the twig, and held it over the flame. When the first side was blackened, he turned the bread over. The toasting created a crisp texture and a smoky flavor. He'd been hungry. The bread was good. He considered another slice but decided against it. He would be gone for a week. He'd save the rest of the bread for later.

He looked again for the canoe. At first he couldn't spot it, then he picked it up again. It was trolling in the other direction. Trolling back to where it had been. Going back and forth along a particularly productive shoreline. Other than the canoe, there was no sign of habitation on the lake. Farther along on the far shoreline, around a spit of land and out of sight from where he stood, he had spied a group of four tiny cabins yesterday. A rustic hunting and fishing lodge, empty for the moment. The summer season over? Other than that, the lake was pristine. The paper company was stingy about the land it leased on these northern Maine lakes.

The twigs were burned out. He gingerly picked up the three rocks that made the sides of the campfire. They were warm but no longer hot enough to burn his fingers. He threw first one and then the two others into the lake. He splashed water onto the flat rock on which he'd built the fire. It sizzled as the water droplets turned to steam. After a few handfuls, the rock and the ashes were cold to his touch. He turned the rock over to hide the blackened surface and slid the stone into the water. Carefully, he looked over the site. One or two remaining broken twigs, out of place on the rocks, he threw into the brush. He wanted to ensure that when he moved on, no sign of his presence would remain. To the careful eye, of course, there was always a sign. A blackened stone. A depression in the leaves. Broken twigs. But at this site, it would be all but impossible to note any sign of his passing.

Satisfied, he looked once more for the canoe across the lake. A minute or more went by before he spotted it. A glint of sun on the wet paddle betrayed it again. The canoe had moved from where it had been trolling. It was farther downwind. He scanned the surface of the lake for other boats. None. That pleased him. He checked that his rod was ready in his boat and then slid the canoe onto the water. Silently he paddled, keeping to the shadow of the shore. Farther out, one could easily be spotted. By staying close to the shoreline, one faded into near invisibility.

From the water, he looked back to where he'd built the fire. Above the jumble of naked rocks between the lapping waves and the brush, it was as if someone had traced a chalk line horizontally along the black granite stones. It marked the summer waterline. Behind that, thick shrubs. Alder in the main. Some unproductive wild blueberry bushes. And then the primary cover of the northern Maine Wilderness: birch down low, spruce above it. Cut hard by the paper companies. The shoreline behind this lake crouched low all around. No tall trees. This cutover Canadian Shield extended from Mt. Katahdin northward forever. South of the lake, a group of four small mountains with a fifth peak, by far the largest and almost perfectly conical from this vantage point, marched west to east toward Mt. Katahdin, where other followers, already arrived, knelt round the high peak in homage. The mountains saved the lake from losing itself in the monotony of the northern back woods, saved the lake from desolation.

He moved slowly, enjoying the sun on his face and soaking in the view. He usually paddled off his left hip, but with a breeze from that side, he had the paddle to starboard. It made it easier to maintain a straight course. Small swirls drifted astern as he dipped and pulled. He watched as the string of swirls receded in his wake. It took but a moment for them to disappear, thereby erasing all sign of his passing. It was why he preferred canoeing to hiking: no matter how careful one might be, hiking left a trail. He searched the lake again for the fisherman he had seen earlier but could not spot him. He had apparently gone elsewhere.

He let the canoe drift, watched as the loons dived and resurfaced. The wavelets against the shore murmured, the sun sparkled on the water. It was a perfect day in the northern Maine Wilderness. In this moment, there was no place on earth he would rather be.

OUT AND BACK

Priests chanting in muted tones, words indistinct, muttering in a strange language. He hovered above them. From there he could see: they were casting dice. Sometimes they shook their heads in apparent disagreement with the numbers on the dice. On other rolls, they mumbled, in accord with what they saw. A face came into focus. His wife. He asked her about the priests. She didn't understand his question. He pointed, but the group had evaporated. His wife faded from his sight.

Vitals. She wanted his vitals. Thermometer in his mouth, pressure cuff on his upper arm, a needle to draw blood. He smiled at her small talk. His son joined in the conversation from where he was sitting in a chair near the window, the sun streaming in behind his elbow. It was a gorgeous day. She arranged the intravenous bags. She had fitted him with two intravenous multiports, one on his right wrist, one on his left. With tubes attached to both his arms and the oxygen feed in his nose, moving around in the bed was awkward, almost impossible. Through the dark he could make out a long tunnel directly in front of his bed. Old bicycles and bicycle parts were heaped high. Behind the tangle of metal, farther down the dark tunnel, a pile of dirty rags. He focused on it. Not rags, an old hag kneeling, covered by a black shawl. He peered. Not an old hag, his cousin. She had died two months ago. She beckoned to him.

His daughter-in-law chatted: the grandchildren were back in school, the holidays were over. She was a nurse, wished to check on me, to assure herself—and me—that I was getting the best of care. She studied the array of intravenous tubing, the display on the monitor. The doctor came in, greeted me. He whispered to my daughter-in-law. She looked surprised. And concerned. A hundred five? The doctor turned to me; he was pleased to see me awake, suggested he move me to the ICU. I would be more comfortable there, he said, and would receive better care. Did I agree? The nurses there had a smaller caseload. I would be in good hands. My daughter-in-law and I exchanged glances, nodded approval. Done, said the doctor, I'll take care of it. You're going to graduate.

Christmas. Lights strung above his head, wires dangling from the top of the tree. Red, green, blue, yellow cascading down. He was right under the tree. His nephew and his niece were with friends, holding hands, dancing around him in a circle. All of them sporting huge tattoos, singing wild songs. He tried to focus. He was lying in bed but the bed was vertical, his legs pointing straight at the ceiling. That could not be. With effort, he could make the illusion disappear, bring his body and the bed back to the horizontal. If he looked away, his body and bed sprang back to the vertical. It made him dizzy.

The park had wrought iron benches, grass, flowers, trees. It was surrounded by cobblestone streets and colonial brick houses. He was dressed in a reenactment uniform, musket in hand. He and the other soldiers marched in formation. He had to urinate; he couldn't hold it another minute. He was wetting himself; his uniform was drenched in urine. Two soldiers were holding him up. He was tangled in wires. His wife was at his side. How had she found him here?

Sorry, sorry, he said to her. I forgot to tell you where I was going. I should have told you! You must have been worried! And my uniform is all wet. Thank you for coming. It's all right, she said. The nurse and I will strip your clothes and the bed. I'm so sorry, I said. I should have told you where I was going! How did you find me? Can I keep my uniform on? Have you met my friends? A wild game was going on. A variety of Ping-Pong. Blazing lights on one side of a huge round table, so bright it blinded him. Figures in white with large mirrors on their foreheads, paddles like mittens instead of hands. Slamming a ball. The remainder of the table was obscured, hidden in the dark. Indistinct figures there, underworld figures. Frightening, wildly overgrown amoebas and paramecia the size of gorillas. They also had paddles and bashed at the ball in the dark, propelling it back into the light. The game frightened him. The two teams were grim, playing for keeps, it seemed. One of the players leaned over him. "Which finger?" she asked. She grabbed one, stuck it with a needle, absconded with a drop of blood.

The room was dark. To the right, in the far corner, he could make out stairs that disappeared into some unknown depth. To where did they descend? He watched furtively, afraid of what might appear from the dark hole. Or worse, that he might be dragged down into an unfathomable underworld. He tried not to look in that direction, but his gaze dragged itself back there, pulled by fear. He managed to sit up. The team gathered around the bed, holding clipboards, studying their notes. Five of them, all specialists in their fields. Pulmonary, cardiac, intravenal, pneumonial, dietary, urinary, I knew not what. Very confusing. I had seen them often, individually, as they made their daily rounds, but was unable to remember who was who. The team was further complicated by each specialist having an alternate who would appear in their stead on different days. Were there as many as twelve of them? They discussed the treatments they had prescribed, analyzed together what changes they might make—stronger doses, other medications. Need to get that fever down, one mumbled. A hundred five. How long has that been? Two days? Way too long. What to do? What would be the next steps? They agreed to meet again in the office at noontime. As they withdrew, they chatted with me, hoped I would be feeling better soon. They had to do something, they said. They had to intervene. They would discuss it together. At their instruction, the nurse inserted an oxygen tube into my nose.

Drowning! Drowning! His wife was screaming. Save him, save him! She was at the pool. He ran as fast as he could. My baby, my baby, she cried. He was out of breath. It's okay, I shouted. It's not me, it's my body, it was on the bottom. I'm not there, I'm here! I explained to her I was okay, I was here, it was just my body down there. I was here, so it was okay. I knew how to swim, I explained. She didn't seem to understand. You've got to eat, she told me. It tasted awful. Cardboard covered with salt. Inedible. How could anyone eat that? The ice cream was okay, but only a bite or two. He didn't want to eat. You have to eat, she said. It was dry as dust in his mouth, it tasted awful.

Early on the twenty-fourth, I awoke, coughing. I'm fine, I said to my wife. I'll go to the store for the seafood as I always do. There would be twenty-three of us for

Christmas Eve. Our children and spouses, our grandchildren, some of our siblings. Every Christmas and New Year's we gathered. We were blessed with such a family, blessed they loved one another, blessed they looked forward to being together to share holidays and birthdays. On every Christmas Eve and New Year's Eve, I would go for the seafood early to be ahead of the crowds. Once the day started in earnest, the line at the counter would be long.

I didn't feel well, a cough and a headache, but I pushed it aside. This was a joyous day, a day for exuberance, a time for family, for togetherness, for love. The grandchildren particularly would be excited. Heaps of gifts under the tree, and Santa would be coming! The little ones would be eating the macaroni and cheese they loved. We, the adults, a smorgasbord of seafood and appetizers, mulled cider, champagne. And, of course, the family we loved. A cup of coffee, a kiss for my wife, and off I drove, headed for the store. Before I could get there, they appeared again. The game was grim. The ball would hurtle out of the bright light into the darkness, disappear for a nanosecond, then come hurtling back. On the bright side of the table, one of the brilliant white figures with paddles for hands and a great round mirror attached to its forehead slammed the ball back toward the dark side, only to have it returned by an indistinct ogre. One would have expected a cheering crowd, a tumult of applause at the ability of the players, but no, the game was played in a grisly silence, as if lives depended on the outcome. Flashing bright light, pitch-black night. The ball in full view and the ball in desolate obscurity. Why so frightening to watch? He tried to make out the ball. What was it made of? It looked like a tiny doll rolled into a miniature sphere. The figures in white were so bright they blinded him. The ogres in the dark could hardly be seen for the shadows, but instinctively he knew they were ugly, disfigured, horrible.

He awoke. He needed to urinate, it was urgent. The empty urine bottle hung on the side of his bed. He scrambled for it, placed it on the mattress at his crotch, under the covers, inserted his penis. At first, he couldn't pee, then it started and he couldn't stop. On and on, and then it was enough. The bottle was almost full; he hung it carefully on the side of his bed. And the sorceress was back. Vitals! Your vitals. She placed a cuff on his arm, rolled a thermometer across his forehead, drew blood from the port at his wrist. She comforted him. It would be fine. She spoke softly to his daughter who was standing at the door. He couldn't make out her words. She shook her head slowly as she disappeared into the hall. A technician came in. His daughter spoke to him; he nodded. Liver function, the technician said. He pressed a wand against his abdomen, rolled it around. His captors tightened the rope around his body. He struggled. He couldn't move his arms. He was tied down. They were kidnapping him. Three women dressed all in white. They didn't understand. They were holding him up, but he was tangled in the ropes. They were screaming at him not to fight them, they were just trying to roll him over. He was determined not to let them kidnap him. His grandson sat quietly in the chair next to his bed. I thought you were at college, I said. No, he replied, I'm still on Christmas break. He asked how I was doing. He didn't seem to comprehend that I was being kidnapped and tied down on a bed. You're a college student, I said. How don't you understand? These guys grabbed me and are trying to kidnap me! They won't let me go! My grandson watched impassively as my captors drove a needle into my arm. I screamed: They're trying to poison me! My grandson smiled gently.

The morning of the thirty-first. He had hardly slept, he felt awful, but he was determined to get to the store early to purchase the seafood they needed to celebrate New Year's Eve. You're in no shape to drive, she said. You fell during the night, there was blood all over. He touched his head; his hair was matted with dry blood. I'll go, he protested. The fall was nothing, I lost my balance in the dark. No, his wife said. You're not well. In the kitchen, my daughter and daughter-in-law sided with my wife. My son had already left to do the shopping in my stead; my wife would drive me to urgent care. We need to leave at once, she said. Given the holiday, they would probably close at noon. All right, I said. My wife wouldn't let me drive. It wasn't yet twelve noon: urgent care was still open. We're in luck, she said. The nurse checked his temperature and blood pressure. He has a fever, she said, dangerously high; his blood pressure is fine. She listened through the stethoscope. We can't handle him here, she told us. His lungs are choked with fluid. He needs to be treated at the hospital. I'll call the emergency room to alert them you're coming. His wife drove him to the hospital, handled the paperwork, checked him in. The ICU? No. He dozed. A room would be ready shortly.

He'd hooked the trailer to the Jeep and driven to the lot not far from the house to buy the Christmas trees. One ten-foot tree for the foyer, a seven-footer for the living room. He was always one of the first customers. He liked to get the trees up and mostly decorated before the Dutch Christmas on December 5. His siblings would be coming. The Dutch Christmas, Sinterklaas, was special. They limited themselves to a few small, funny gifts to fill the *klompen*: no need for extensive shopping. It was the only time each year the four of them, he and his three siblings, managed to get together. Simple. But terrific to be able to see each other. His son and two of his grandsons would be at the house to help him erect the two trees. With them, it would be a quick and easy job. Some years he had only his wife to help. With just the two of them, it was a daunting task to get the larger tree up and stabilized. With a few of the younger generation to assist, it was easy as pie and became a work of love. Lots of jokes, a few cups of coffee and laughter, scads of laughter.

She was waving to him. Beckoning. It was hard to make her out, far down the tunnel in the pitch black, hidden in heaps of rags and a tangle of metal. She called, but he couldn't hear her voice. It was clear she wanted him to come. How could she call? She had died some weeks ago. He was pulled toward her; he couldn't resist. He panicked, held tight to the bars at his side. She called. Come. Come!

The tree was stabilized. The next task was to string lights. That was his job. He had set up the ten-foot stepladder he always used. Once he had the lights strung, others could add the decorations: his wife, his daughter, his grandchildren. Everyone who came to the house during the days leading to Christmas would add a few baubles. Everyone had a favorite decoration or two. Everyone would add a touch of love. But first, the Christmas Angel. He set her gently on the very top of the tree.

He shifted his eyes away from the far-right corner of the room. No light there. Only blackness, stairs leading down. That corner of the room frightened him. Shadows shifted there, lurked in the darkness. He tried to look away. Shadowy figures crept out of the darkness, sneaked toward his bed. They had him then, cords tightening around him. He pulled away. They had pinned his wrist. He tugged. Pain! They had him at the top of the steps, they were pulling him down into the hole. He was sliding, sliding down into an underworld. He cried out. He didn't want to disappear. The shadows pulled at his feet. It was black, he couldn't see. He struggled not to disappear. He was falling, slipping; he was being swallowed by the hole. Laughter gurgled up from below. They had him! It was over! His wrist hurt, blood on his arm. He called for help. They pushed the shadows away, and he was struggling with two ladies. It will be all right! All right! He was tied all about. His wife protecting him. She and a nurse fighting the intruders. Don't fight us, they said. We'll have you untangled in a moment. The nurse was upset: I had ripped the port out of my wrist where it had been fastened. Lie down, they said. I tried to explain why I was fighting—they were pulling me into the hole! It's all right, they said. They didn't understand. Nobody understood me. I tried to explain. Lie down, they said. My wrist hurt where the shadows had clawed at me. The oxygen tubes pulled at my ears.

She smiled. Chocolate chip cookies! For me! Next to her—was it her sister?—the woman took his hand, singled out one of his fingers, pricked him with a needle. He was being poisoned! Don't. Don't! He tried to scream. No, she said, not poison, diabetes. She smiled, proud of herself, stole away a drop of his blood. A witch! She would cast a spell on him! Someone was rubbing his leg. Up and down. What? A wand, he said. Good, I said. A magic wand. Can I make a wish? Yes, make me better. I want to get better. I dozed. I'm checking for clots, he said. He kept on, rubbing my leg. Fine story, I thought, but if rubbing my leg with a wand might help, go for it. I wanted to talk but forgot what I wanted to say.

She pulled the bedclothes down. Pinched my abdomen. Keep away! Leave me alone. No, no, no! She was a smooth talker. Before I knew it, she had stabbed me in the stomach, pushed the plunger. Just to be safe, she said. Before she had put back the blankets, her companion was after my vitals. Hmmm. Hardly any fever. She slid a pair of slippers on my feet and cuffs around my leg. Plugged it in. The gentle pressure on my lower legs was accompanied by a rolling massage. Soothing. I fell asleep.

It was an undersized watering pitcher. Clear plastic, blue stripes on the side, to measure the right quantity of water for each indoor plant. No, I was told, put the spout in your mouth. I started to blow. Inhale, I was told. Move the marker up the cylinder by inhaling. Ten times. It will be good for your lungs. I did as instructed. I need to defecate, I said. The nurse helped me out of bed to sit on the toilet chair. With the tangle of wires and tubes, getting from the bed to the toilet chair was a major task.

Priests chanting in muted tones, words indistinct, muttering in a strange language. He hovered above them. From there he could see: they were casting dice. Sometimes they shook their heads in disagreement, argued about the numbers on the dice. On other rolls, they mumbled, in accord with what they saw. He was in the park dressed in a Civil War uniform, musket in hand. He and the other soldiers stood at attention. His uniform was drenched in blood. Two soldiers grabbed him, pinned his arms to his side. His wife was running toward him. Thank you, thank you, he said to her. You've saved me! She laid him down on a wrought iron bench. She called a nurse. She stripped off his uniform. His wife kissed him, said she had to go.

His cousin waved to him. He pretended not to see her. She called. No, he said to himself, no. I don't want to see you. You're dead! Go away. Leave me alone! He was terrified of the dark tunnel. He closed his eyes. He managed to make her disappear.

The doctors were there, all five of them. We think you're ready to leave the ICU, they said. We have a room ready for you. Okay? I looked at my wife, she nodded assent. Absolutely, I replied. Can I be discharged? I asked. I'd like to go home. Not yet, not yet. We need to get you off oxygen. She held the belt behind him, at the small of his back, ready to right him if he stumbled. She had asked, did he want to try to walk to his new room or did he want a wheelchair? Walk, he said. Are you sure? I've never yet let anyone walk out of the ICU. Determined: I'll walk. She pushed the button; the automatic doors opened outward, toward freedom. He walked, stepped through the opening. A few yards down the corridor stood his brother. He raised his arms in a great victorious V. "You've escaped!" He gritted his teeth, smiled. I've escaped. Freed. Liberated! He continued to walk. Are you okay? she asked. We'll take a left at the end of the corridor. He was walking, no problem. And now past the elevators, just a few more doors. Yes, said his brother, I landed an hour ago, came straight to the hospital. A few days ago, it sounded as if I might not be in time. Now you're walking! And no longer in the ICU! It's so good to see you.

Two days later, when the doctor came by, he inquired how I felt, asked if I wanted to be released. It was Friday. Monday would be a holiday. Did I wish to stay for the long weekend, recuperate a bit more? Or did I feel up to leaving? Out, out, I wanted out! I'd already been here almost three weeks! If I wasn't released this afternoon, I would be here until Tuesday. I'd been here far too long. I'll sign you out, said the doctor. The staff will process you. The wait seemed an eternity. Paperwork. Medicaid needed to be notified. Oxygen tanks needed to be delivered to the house. It was now five p.m. Could all the formalities be completed this late on a Friday? Eight o'clock, still needed the paperwork. Waiting, waiting. Now nine p.m. Would it really happen? Did I really want out? asked the staff. My God, of course. Out, out! Just before ten I was released.

His wife drove. And then, there was the house. Freedom! It was done! He was home! A miracle. The hospital was left behind. He was inside, trailing fifty feet of plastic tubing attached to the pump that forced oxygen into his nose, but he was free. It was a long night: every twenty minutes he had to urinate, he had to rid himself of the quarts of the fluids they had poured into him.

Morning! How beautiful, the sun streaming through their bedroom windows. And now time to recuperate, to rebuild his strength. My, how it was good to be home! Across the living room and back, into the kitchen and out. He needed to move. He wanted to regain his strength. His legs thin sticks, he might as well have just escaped from Auschwitz. His arms no better: skin wrinkled and hanging loose. No muscle, nothing more than bone. His wife was as relieved as he was that he was home. His hospitalization was as stressful for her as it was for him. Possibly more: she hadn't even had a bed to sleep on! With a smile from ear to ear she served him breakfast. It was good to be home, good to be together again. At ten a.m. the nurse practitioner was scheduled to check on him.

He sat for a while and then worked his way up the stairs

and back down. Hard work. He had weighed 143 pounds on entering the hospital. After all the fluids they had pumped into him he was a bloated 158 pounds the day before his discharge. Twenty-four hours later, he weighed 122 pounds. How was it possible for his frame, already sinewy and without fat, to shed twenty-one pounds from its normal weight? He would need to regain his strength. He tried to do a sit-up. Not possible. Rolled over. A pushup? No way. It was a bit of a struggle, but he managed to get up from the floor, walked again across the room and back, timed himself to do ten minutes before taking a break. Life was coming back in focus.

The doorbell rang. Ouch! How could this be a health professional? Five-foot-two and three-hundred-fifty pounds. She waddled in, chose a big chair, lowered herself into it—carefully. Clearly, she had broken a chair or two in her life. For a half hour she never moved a muscle, except for those in her tongue and lips. Told me about her kids, how tough her life was. Getting up to leave? For a few minutes, I thought she would remain planted in the chair for the rest of her life. After huffing and puffing and heaving, she was finally erect. She had given me no instructions, asked no questions about my condition. She had come apparently for no reason other than to confirm I was using the oxygen twenty-four hours a day. She had been pleased to see I was tethered to the oxygen tube.

How good it was to loll around the house, to sit at our kitchen table, for my wife and me to remake acquaintance. It was as if I'd been away for a year or two. We had both been frightened. Slowly the fright ebbed and we took up the loose ends of our life. She filled me in on the happenings of the New Year's Eve festivities we had missed, and on the three weeks I had been away. Well, not so much "away" physically, but "away" mentally. Everyone had been worried for me: some had already been making plans for paying my bills and for arranging my funeral. Upon my release from the hospital, the whole of the extended family had breathed a comforting sigh of relief and had returned to their day-to-day routines.

Two days later it was the physical therapist. Young, energetic, optimistic; a breath of fresh air in comparison to the nurse practitioner who had preceded her. I came to show you what you should be doing, she said, to get you started. Your wife said you had been doing some walking and some light exercises. That's good, but be careful you don't overdo it. Walk? Ten minutes every hour, inside, at a slow pace. Have you tried stairs? she asked. I climbed the steps to the second story, pulling on the banister to aid my legs. I've been doing the stairs every two or three hours I told her. And I've been doing some knee lifts. Squats? No, not full squats, but a few half squats while holding to the table. Sit on that chair, she instructed, pointing to a straight-backed kitchen chair. Let's see how many times you can straighten from a sitting position to a standing position and back down to sit. She timed me. Almost twenty-five reps in thirty seconds, she said; it would normally be a month or more to get to where you are now. It's Wednesday morning, you were released Friday? Four days? That's good progress. She suggested additional exercises. I'll check on you in a week, she said. Given where you are now, that will be it for me. From there you can go it on your own.

Two days later, he was able to discard the oxygen tube. He was now doing curls, though he couldn't do them with weights. But bit by bit, he could do more. Walking outside was almost impossible at the start. Initially a hundred yards on gravel took forty-five minutes and was a lesson in pain management. A few more days, and he was walking a quarter mile, slowly, painfully, with his sister by his side. God it was good to be out in the open air, under the trees rising high above, feeling the breeze, chatting with someone he loved. The next weekend his wife invited their children and grandchildren for a Saturday barbeque. How wonderful, the kisses and the smiles! The hospital was truly behind him.

At the six-week follow-up visit, the doctor said he was pleased to see me. We thought we'd lost you, he said. We thought we'd lost you. I'm pleased to see you. You almost slipped away. You're looking well. I'm glad our team won.

THE PSYCH MAJOR

Christmas 1963

The decorations are starting to make me feel more like Christmas. Funny how at college it was hard to believe that Christmas was almost here but now that I'm nearing home I can feel it. It's the excitement in the streets and the people getting off and being kissed and hugged and the people getting on with packages and smiles as they think of who—no, whom—they're about to see. Even the Negroes in the streets look happy. Oops, I should remember, it's Blacks! I do hope Mom and Dad like the gifts but I don't have to hope about Cathy; she's sure to love that dress. I'm sort of excited and also scared some. They'll all be happy to see me and be bubbling with a thousand questions, but I will have to be careful not to sound too liberal or modern in front of Mom or Dad. They'd never believe I believe so many different things, that I've changed so much. Dad would shoot me if he knew I was against protective tariffs, even on cotton goods and cane sugar. Or that I think government support of farm crops should be abolished. Worse, that I think Governor Wallace's segregation stance is wrong! And Mom would die if she knew I had petted and that I thought that maybe, with the guy you're going to marry anyway, it might be all right to have intercourse and that a lot of the girls sleep with lots of guys. It makes me wonder about beliefs and mores and everything. Kind of makes me think that woman, whoever she was again, Meade, Margaret Meade it was, that did all the research on all those primitive tribes and discovered that what some thought was right others thought was wrong, like polygamy and polyandry and monogamy, might be right. Down here I believed a whole lot of things and boom, I get put in college, just like being raised by another tribe, and now I believe a whole lot of other things. Maybe they're no more right than what I used to think, than what Mom and Dad think, but I think they are. At least now I realize that just like in math, one has to attempt to deduce one's opinions from basic premises, whereas before I just believed because I was brought up like that. I wonder whether I could make Cathy understand that; she's bright enough. I wonder for instance if I could explain why classical music is more complex than pop. She'd probably understand in a vague way but not be interested. I'll have to be careful with all of them, not to shock them too much with my way-out ideas. It'll be hard enough trying to explain why I'm going to major in psych when they all expect me to be a math major. At least I bet that's what they all expect, though it does not necessarily follow that because I won my scholarship in a math contest that I'll be a mathematician. They won't like psychology if I tell them I'm taking it because I've become so interested in conditioning. Was I ever conditioned! It's just something you never think about before college, how your beliefs are merely conditioned responses. For me just like Mom's and Dad's, for some of the girls at school the opposite of their parents because they're rebelling. But 90 percent of responses are conditioned and all but impossible to change. Take sex. If some guy tried to make love to me I'd probably be petrified and yet I can see why it's not bad, why it would even be good for you, better than petting and petting until you are frustrated. Still, if I slept with a guy I'd feel terrible, I'm sure, even if I wanted and was going to marry him. And that's ridiculous but it would take me a long time to get over my guilt. Why? Because Mom and Dad have got me so conditioned that I can't change, not even using reason. Or at least it would take me a long while. But I can't try to explain all that about conditioning, Dad would probably argue he has a good reason for everything, that he isn't conditioned at all. Like being a Baptist, for instance. He would probably say we were Baptists because it's God's church. He wouldn't admit that the main reason is that his parents were Baptists and that their parents were Baptists. And even more fundamental, if I asked him why he believed in God he'd just say because there is a God. He'd bellow if I tried to point out that most probably he believed because he was told to when he was a kid. Not that there aren't good arguments but that's something I will have to do some reading and thinking about. Those philosophy professors sure aren't afraid to question whether or not there is a God. I'd never met anyone, anyone, in Masonville who would dare mention that God might not exist. I'm not sure now whether I believe because I was conditioned or because I have good reasons. I mean I have good reasons but maybe I'm just rationalizing because I was conditioned to want to believe. That's another subject I will havc to avoid, it seems like I have to avoid nearly everything, Mom and Dad might make me quit college if they thought college was putting wild ideas in my head, as Mom says. And I'd hate to have to leave. I wasn't sure in September whether I'd like college or not. After all most of the kids from my class didn't go and if they did they didn't go up north but just went to U of A, but it's the best thing that ever happened. I mean they used to call me a bookworm and all that but wow, now I read twice as much and still most of the girls seem to know more but I think I'll catch up to them. Most of them have just had better teachers and schools but are lazy though some, like my roommate, I will have to tell Cathy about Janet's clothes, are really smart and I'll never be that good but I know I'm no slouch. Besides, they're all really impressed when they find out I won a nationwide math contest though a lot of that was luck, I think. And the best thing is that being a bookworm no longer makes me an outcast like down here where I never even went out 'cause the guys were afraid 'cause they thought I was too smart. Wow, was that Jonathan at that last cocktail party ever nice and I hope, I sure do hope he will ask me out after Christmas. That's another thing I can't mention: cocktails. Dad would tan my hide if he ever found out that I drink. Maybe I should tell him just to see how he reacts. That would be hilarious! Probably not a good idea. Now there's a stellar example of pure conditioning, though he'd never ever admit it. He'd just say that liquor is the devil's brew and point to the town drunk and say see what happens when you "imbibe," as he says, and all my arguing that one does not have to drink to excess wouldn't even be heard. Not that I'll argue with Dad, there's no sense to it for he wouldn't listen and it would just create hard feelings. That's why I'm not going to mention politics or religion or drinking, not to mention not mentioning sex. Not because I'm afraid but I know it would start a mean argument and everybody would end up mad and it wouldn't have proved anything because I'm not about to change my views and they won't change theirs. So, circumspection will be the word for this vacation. At least I haven't changed completely in three months, at least I still know better than to argue with Dad, something Cathy never has learned. But I have changed a lot, I guess, or at least changed some of my opinions. Janet's played a large part in that, I've never met anyone who tries so hard to think everything out bit by bit and who then acts in accordance with her rational decisions. And I'll have to admit most of her conclusions are good, and surprisingly enough thinking things out hasn't made her at all cold or masculine. She has some of the sexiest clothes ever. She sure has changed me a lot, though everything in college has helped, and it's been fun arguing with her about sex and liquor and religion and politics and clothes and civil rights. That's another thing I will have to be careful not to mention. Would Dad and Mom ever scream and holler if they heard me say that civil rights is more than just good schools for the Negroes, Blacks I mean, that civil rights is integrated schools and integrated public facilities of all sorts. Even Cathy wouldn't speak to me, or maybe I should say especially Cathy. I can just hear her with a "me sit next to a nigger in school?!" and I guess I couldn't blame her. Three months ago I wouldn't have been able to consider integrated schools so it's no wonder that she, being my sister and thinking like me or I guess I should say being conditioned like me and being in high school and never having been out of Alabama, can't conceive of integrated schooling. Even I have to watch myself, like when I forget and say nigger instead of Black and I know it will take me a long time to be able to accept them as complete equals. I could never think of marrying one though I see why Janet says that interracial marriage is the ultimate proof of nonprejudice. I'm just too conditioned for that. It will take me years even to be able to dance with a Black, there I got it right, maybe I'll never be able to. But all that isn't too important, I just have to keep forcing myself to accept them, little by little by little. It's like when dresses started getting short a couple of years ago, at first I thought they really looked queer, but the longer I kept convincing myself they looked elegant the more elegant they looked. So I will just have to keep trying to convince myself that Negroes oops there I go again, are just like everyone else, some good, some bad just as Janet says. Maybe lots of stupid ones but that's not because they're Blacks, it's because they have poor backgrounds and bad schools, but still there's lots of whites like that and I feel differently about them. And that's what prejudice is, and that's what I'm going to have to work on, getting rid of thinking of them as different. Even Janet admits she isn't completely free of prejudice, she says she often feels like she's being too nice, kind of solicitous towards the Negroes she meets, oops there I go again, but then she thinks it's because she knows so few that they stand out when she meets them. After all there isn't one Black in the whole college, or maybe a couple but I don't have any in class and there aren't any in any of the sororities, so it's no wonder they stand out. It is kind of funny seeing so many niggers in the streets again, as a matter of fact it's kind of nice being down here with the weather not so cold and the sun out though it's not hot. I can hardly wait to get home. I wonder if Mom's going to have turkey for Christmas dinner. I'll bet she is, and I bet Cathy has got a new boyfriend, I wonder if she's thought about college. As a junior she ought to but I guess she isn't very interested but maybe if she's going with a guy who's going to U of A she'll go too. She ought to go, she's smart as a whip but I guess she'll never make a good student, she's too boy crazy and subconsciously believes that if she were to study she would no longer be attractive. She probably got that from watching me have troubles, being called a brain and all. That's kind of why I wish she'd go north, she'd find out that there are plenty of guys who like smart women. Maybe I should get Janet to come down and visit, maybe at Easter. If Cathy saw how good-looking Janet was and how terrific her clothes were and knew how many boyfriends she had and then discovered how smart she was maybe Cathy'd decide to go to college up north. But I guess that wouldn't do any good 'cause Dad and Mom wouldn't be able to afford to send her away and she'd never get a scholarship. The best plan's to find her a guy at U of A and then she'd go there and maybe learn something, though probably not much, but it would be better than nothing. I'll tell her about all the parties at college and about how well-dressed the girls are, then she'll go. That girl out there, I'll bet she's in college, I kind of like her heels and the skirt with that slit. She's about the best-dressed on the platform, except maybe for that woman but she doesn't have as cute a figure. Everybody seems to be getting off the bus here, I'm kind of glad that old man who was sitting next to me left, he kind of smelled. Maybe some handsome guy will sit next to me, maybe somebody going to Masonville and he'll date me during vacation, but hoping for that is kind of like believing in fairies. There comes a guy but I guess that's his wife getting on the bus, not much hope there and he's too old anyway. I hope those sailors behind that nigger and her little boy, there I go again, Black I mean, don't sit next to me, they're usually fresh and try to be wise guys. Damn, she's going to put her kid here! I hope he doesn't smell and here's my first test. Remember that he's just like any other kid and don't panic, look out the window if you have to, just sitting next to you isn't going to hurt, not one bit, don't edge away like you're afraid of the plague, sit in the middle of the seat, relax, take it easy. Like Janet says there's really no difference, he's just got skin a little darker than yours, and she's right, you can't smell a thing and so what if he's a little black boy, he isn't going to bite. Well so far so good, step number one has just been forced on me and I'm passing, but relaxed I sure am not. I'm taut as a clothesline draped with wet sheets and there's even sweat on my palms but at least I've got control, though I'm awfully glad there's an armrest between us. Now to see if I can lean back and relax, that's better, I just hope the bus doesn't lurch too much. Good, the driver's starting slowly so the kid won't fall in my lap, that would be too much, I don't think I could keep from screaming. Janet will be happy to know I'm on the way, though it will be a long time before I can dance with one. Sitting next to this one is already bad enough, but at least I'm trying and that's a good start. I sure am conditioned, though; I'll bet Janet would never understand how scared I am of having this kid next to me. He's pretty small and the white palms with the black around them look weird but I don't care what Janet says, his face is ugly as sin. Luckily he's not climbing around or I'd be in a panic that he might jump onto my lap, he must be tired, he looks awfully tired and already he's nodding, half asleep. I'm going to have to sit next to more nig—Blacks I mean, and get used to them before I try any social situations. Have to do it slowly. This kid's hair is really kinky and the scalp under the hair shows. It's kind of revolting. He must be sleepy. My God his head is going to slide over to my shoulder. My God. I hope it doesn't slide. It's going to, already it's sliding. Easy now. It's just like any other kid, it's no different. No different. Don't slide, head. Don't. I'm not ready, oh God it's going to touch me and I'm not ready oh don't don't oh GOD!

* * *

"What happened back here?"

"Get away, everybody, get away. Make a little room. It's all right, driver. This girl just fainted. Had some sort of fit. She's sitting peaceable like when suddenly she screamed and sort of jumped and fell out of her seat. Must have had a fit or something. She'll come to in a moment. You go ahead, stop maybe at the next service station for some water. I'll take care back here. I'm a doctor, she'll be all right. Just fainted."

TWO WORLDS

The sun brooded over the pondering sea. Sky and water were nothing but blue. No clouds, no foam. The *Tari* thrummed gently, proving she moved. All else was still. To port, the rocks and scrub of the Turkish coast could be seen clearly, yet it was another world. To those on board the *Tari,* it did not exist.

The heat, the quiet. It was siesta time on board. The rusted *Tari* and its thrumming engine had drugged the passengers. On deck, they lay as if doped in the shade of cranes or winches. Below decks, they baked on cots. Two chickens, tied to the railing, squatted low. Their eyes were filmed. Nothing moved.

Aft, under canvas hung for shade, squatted three men. Their movements were slow; they communicated little. When they spoke, it was in grunts and gestures. They had no common language. They traveled together on the *Tari* by chance, each coming from a different country. Sharing a watermelon, they sucked the red flesh, spat the seeds into the sea.

Languidly, one of the men gestured overboard; the others turned their heads to see. All three drifted to the rail. In the water, facedown, a body floated. The body of a man. It swirled into the *Tari*'s wake. One of the men spat a seed in that direction. The three grunted and gestured. What should they do? One man lurched forward. He disappeared into the *Tari*'s wheelhouse.

After a few minutes the *Tari* changed course, beginning to circle. The captain had decided to arc back in search of the body.

After some time, the ship returned to where her wake still showed in the seas. The captain followed the wake on its old course, the men looking overboard. Some of the other passengers had roused themselves. They noted that the *Tari* had changed course and asked why. They too scanned the sea.

Despite the many eyes searching the glassy surface, unblemished but for the few bubbles marking the boat's prior wake, no one spotted the body. The ship continued on its course parallel to the coast; the captain did not circle back a second time. The sun beat down on the ocean and the ship. The passengers sought out shade, hiding from the unbearable heat; the three men returned aft to the shelter of their canvas. One cut three more slices of the melon, and they sucked impassively at the red flesh. The chickens slept on in the oppressive heat. The coast, the other world, slipped by as the *Tari* thrummed gently.

AUTUMN

He drove slowly along the dry dirt road. The surface was a washboard, but Dan was not driving slowly because of the bumps. During the summer he would have bounded along this section. The road steepened, then flattened as the high spot was reached. He pulled over. It was where he and his brother had picked strawberries in early June, tiny beads packed with flavor, which had stained their fingers and palms bright red. Back in the woods was the gold mine that they had found later in the day. Just a shaft lined with the trunks of hard oaks, half filled with water. It had been a thrill finding it. Across the road down into the field was where he had chipped for beryl crystals in late June. And farther, where the fields met the now red and orange oaks, he had picked blueberries in August. Nearly twenty quarts he had picked. Then, hot and itchy, he had gone for a long swim in Winnipesaukee's waters. The surface hot, but the cool water underneath reminded one that it was not always summer.

It was not always summer. Dan felt it for the first time. Summer would go. Winter would come. For some reason as he gazed across the fields, the realization of the coming of winter hit him hard, as if it were a physical pain rising from his abdomen into his chest, staggering him, choking him. The emotion was so strong, he felt he had been assaulted. He shook his head, forced himself to take a few deep breaths; within a few minutes the pain and light-headedness passed. The sun was hot, even though the heat did not brood over the grass and under the trees as it did in mid-July. The northwest wind—in summer it was westerly—was cool. It rustled the leaves, which were not green and dry from the heat, but dead. A brown had crept into the hard yellow of the field grass. It was unmistakable, he thought: summer was dead, winter would soon claim its due.

Dan continued to gaze across the sweep of the field, looked beyond to the red and orange oaks mingling with the evergreen of the hemlocks, to the edge of Winnipesaukee. He searched the surface of the lake but could see no boats. In early June, there were no boats; they were all still in dry dock. It was a great time for sailing and swimming. The water was cold but warming after the winter. There were no annoying buzz-saw motors because the summer folk had not yet come. Now it was quiet again, most of the boats already in dry dock ahead of the coming winter. The summer folk were gone. The hot sun was gone. The summer, his vacation, were slipping softly but quickly into the past. His brother had left back in late June. It would soon be his time to depart.

Why the always parting, the passing of the good times? His friends at UNH—he had bid them good-bye in June. Most of them he would never see again. And four years before, it had been a painful good-bye to

Detroit. Not that he loved Detroit itself, but he had loved high school, the close-knit group of friends, the guys on his teams. UConn had been an enormous change for him, a whole new life. A new city, a new state, a new way of life, making new friends, highs and lows, laughs and tears, and then the inevitable good-byes. Of the two lives, he had loved high school the most; but when memories of those days bubbled up, they seemed to come from a different him, from a different person, from a different life. He had loved fall the most: football, hunting, and, of course, Billy-Jean. Fridays, there had always been an evening game under the lights. The nerves before the game, the thrill of winning, even the dying inside after losing had been a life in itself. The sore muscles told of tackles and blocks. Proved contact. Proved there was life. The after-game dance, usually just quietly sitting with Billy-Jean, sipping lemonade.

And then at midnight, a good-night kiss, and he and Bassman would pile into the car already loaded with decoys. The night drive to Saginaw Bay, thinking of Billy-Jean. A little hurt at the parting, but a quiet joy of knowing he would return Sunday night. Out on the lake long before dawn, floating the decoys and then sleeping in the fog. The landing ducks jolted him into complete wakefulness. Those times were also past. It saddened him. The upside was he had already lived two full lives; the downside, he had died twice. What would this third life bring?

Here in New Hampshire, the country was lovely. But lonely. Swimming, working, and golf had been his summer. A little sailing, but now that he thought about it, once his brother had departed, he had done everything alone. Golf he had started only because he could find no one who played tennis. But swimming and golf were a wonderful summer. Now it was nearly gone. A few more rounds on the empty course. The water was already too cold for more than a quick dip. Sailing was not much fun if there were no other boats to race. Funny, sailing alone in June he enjoyed. But then he was looking forward to the summer, not feeling the sadness of things past. He'd go out on the water once more. He would have one last sail. One more before he left.

The sadness of things past. One should leave that sadness and look forward. Forget the summer. Think of the hunting season, of skiing. Hard, he thought. He could think ahead, but the sadness, the loss, stayed in the stomach. This was what makes one old. Young as he was, already he knew how it was to get old. The always parting, the passing of good times, the leaving of friends, never quite sure they'd ever meet again. The sadness in the stomach. He might look ahead, but he could never forget. The sadness always seeps in. Summer cannot be forgotten. The pain that had welled within him at the thought of the coming winter rose again. A bottomless nostalgia—how could nostalgia cause such pain in his chest? He breathed deeply to dispel the sensation.

He looked toward the brambles in hopes of finding a late blackberry. No luck. Slowly, he started the car down the hill, down toward the lake where the boats were kept. One last sail, he thought, smiling wryly, before autumn ceded to the cold death of winter. Behind him, he left the down-sweeping field and the red and orange oaks in the distance. He liked that the oaks were mixed with hemlocks. The hemlocks were always green.

He parked the car, walked toward the small patch of beach. Before he got there, he stumbled, caught himself, stopped. He was tired, it had been a busy summer. After two or three deep breaths, he continued. During the summer, there were ten or more identical rental boats here on the bit of sandy beach, all sized for a single sailor or at most a crew of two. Now only one sailboat remained, the others carefully mothballed for the winter. No choice. This one was a bit battered, but it would do. As he leaned over to push the boat across the sand toward the water, he felt light-headed. He paused, grasped the gunnel for support, noted the chipped and faded name on the transom. The letters were hard to read, but he was able to make them out. The boat was named the *Char*. Appropriate, he thought. Named after a fish.

He started forward. As the bow reached the water's edge, he advanced more slowly, until the whole of the boat but for the stern was afloat. Before he straightened, he looked more closely at the letters on the transom and realized he had been mistaken. There had once been two additional letters, now faded and flaked off, that he had not noticed. He rubbed the area with his finger. An *a* it seemed, or, given the rounded top, more probably an *e* or an *o*. It wasn't clear. And the last letter even more difficult to decipher. He studied the spot, rubbed it again. It seemed to be an *m* or maybe an *n*. He couldn't tell. Too bad. He rather liked *Char* as a name.

A flair of movement made him look heavenward; a dozen or more swallows flew wildly above, soaring and diving in exuberance. They were pausing here for a few days before migrating south. Winter would shortly be upon them, and they'd be leaving soon. Watching their flight, he was taken by a desire to fly with them when they left.

He pushed the sailboat into the water, boarded, and hoisted the sail. As he pulled away from the beach, the shadow of the sail on the hull caught his eye and for a moment it made him think he was not sailing alone. Pretending he had a companion on board, he spoke to the shadow, and the two of them agreed to set course for the far shore. It gave him comfort to be joined. Since it would be his last sail, he looked back to the beach as they pulled away, wanting one more time to enjoy the scene of the beach with the mountains rising behind. He had truly loved his summer here. New Hampshire was a paradise. It was hard to depart. He gazed back at the receding shore. All good things, he thought, friends, love, life … He shook his head sorrowfully. All good things come to an end.

LIKE GOD

A play in one act

Characters

Girl One, also known as **Ms. Timid.** She is four years old and dressed prettily in a colorful snow jacket and short dress with long knee socks. She has long blond hair and blue eyes.

Boy One, also known as **Mr. Know-It-All**. He is five, but big for his age. He wears corduroy pants, a battered winter jacket, and has a baseball cap on backward.

Girl Two, also known as **Ms. Cynic**. She is dressed sloppily in slacks and an old boy's winter jacket. Ms. Cynic is a young lady who already at the age of four finds life boring.

Boy Two, also known as **Rodin**. A cute boy with floppy hair and dressed well without quite being a Little Lord Fauntleroy. The look of a thinker hangs about him. He speaks slowly, seemingly weighing his words. He obviously has educated parents who do not speak down to him, and he obviously parrots their adult language as if it were his own. Hence he appears far older than his five or so years.

Girl Three, also known as **The Girl Next Door.** She is dressed in the style of the day, but without taste for she is one of those creatures who does exactly what everyone else does for no reason other than that everyone does it.

Boy Three, also known as **The Boy Next Door.** He is also dressed in the style of the day and for the same reason as The Girl Next Door. He is not outward going, has no spark, and will turn into one of those adults who never think for themselves.

(The curtain rises on a darkened stage. After a few moments of silence, Christmas carols are heard in the distance. It is the sound of piped music coming from loudspeakers outside city stores. Gradually, the lights of a decorated Christmas tree appear on stage until the tree is fully lit. It is resplendent with Christmas decorations. But for the tree, the stage is bare. Ms. Timid enters left as the stage lightens. She walks cautiously to the middle of the stage. She is obviously timid and it takes her a few moments to say anything. Then, in impish good humor mixed with childish embarrassment, she greets the audience with a "Hi" and a little wave before running off stage.)

MR. KNOW IT ALL

(Swaggering onto the stage with his hands in his trouser pockets.)

Hi everybody.

(Points offstage in the direction of Ms. Timid.)

She's a little nervous 'cause it's her first play. I guess ya can't blame 'er. She was supposed to tell ya 'bout the play, but I guess I'll hafta. It's a play about Christmas, but ya probably figured that 'cause of the tree and the music. This is a city, no special city, just the one where I an' all those other kids live. That music comes from some stores where our parents are shopping.

(Points to different parts of the stage.)

This is a playground. Ya know, with swings an' seesaws an' one of those things ya push around an' jump on, and a sandbox and stuff, and all around is a big wire fence. We come here all the time to play. I live pretty nearby. It's all right for a place to live, but it's kinda dirty. Ya know, sooty and with that smoggy junk in the air like smoke.

(He pauses.)

Well, I guess that's about all there is to tell.

(Beckons offstage.)

C'mon kids, it's time to start. C'mon.

(From offstage comes the sound of children's laughter and running feet. Ms. Timid, Ms. Cynic, The Girl Next Door, Rodin, and The Boy Next Door run onstage. Jumping and laughing, they mill together, then step forward one by one to greet the audience.)

MS. TIMID

(Less timid than before but still shy)

Hi.

MS. CYNIC

(Waves nonchalantly.)

Hi, everyone.

RODIN

Good evening. I trust you are all well.

THE GIRL NEXT DOOR

Hello, everyone.

THE BOY NEXT DOOR

Hello.

MR. KNOW-IT-ALL

Now we've all met ya, so we can get started.

(The children run to various parts of the stage. The girls play patty-cake and sit as if in a sandbox. Rodin goes to the Christmas tree to ponder the needles and ornaments. Left together are Mr. Know-It-All and The Boy Next Door.)

MR. KNOW-IT-ALL

(Speaking to the audience since he likes to impress adults.)

When we were out there (points offstage), we were talking, and ya know what? He (nods scornfully at The Boy Next Door) really believes there's a Santa Claus!

(The audience is now forgotten, and the children speak only to each other.)

THE BOY NEXT DOOR

There is! Everyone says there is! Even my daddy says there is!

MR. KNOW-IT-ALL

Pooh! Santa Claus is just for kids. Kid stuff. When ya grow up, ya don't believe in Santa. (Haughtily.) I don't believe.

THE BOY NEXT DOOR

I do. There is a Santa Claus. Ask anyone.

MR. KNOW-IT-ALL

Okay. (They run over to where the girls sit on the edge of the sandbox. Mr. Know-It-All points at The Boy Next Door and laughs scornfully.) He believes in Santa Claus and I don't.

THE BOY NEXT DOOR

(Defensively, less sure.)

There is a Santa Claus!

MR. KNOW-IT-ALL

Isn't.

THE BOY NEXT DOOR

Is.

MR. KNOW-IT-ALL

Isn't.

THE BOY NEXT DOOR

Is.

MR. KNOW-IT-ALL

(Holding up hand.)

Okay, you'll see. I bet the girls don't believe. (The two boys glance at the three girls.) Right?

(The girls don't reply, stunned by a question they had never considered.)

MS. TIMID

(Finally.)

Mama says there's a Santa Claus so there must be. (Suddenly recalling.) Besides, I've seen him.

THE GIRL NEXT DOOR

So have I and he left me presents last year.

THE BOY NEXT DOOR

See! (Makes a face at Mr. Know-It-All.) I told you!

MR. KNOW-IT-ALL

(To Ms. Cynic.)

How 'bout you?

MS. CYNIC

(She shrugs. She is uninterested.)

I dunno. (Speaking to the three believers.) Just 'cause you believe doesn't make Santa real.

(Rodin joins the group. Mr. Know-It-All turns to him.)

MR. KNOW-IT-ALL

An' you?

RODIN

(He shrugs too, not in uncaring but in unknowing. He has the uncertainty of one who weighs a question carefully and understands the merit of both sides. He speaks with a tone far beyond his years.)

On the one hand, my father says there is a Santa Claus. On the other hand, as my mom says, my father has been known to be wrong.

MR. KNOW-IT-ALL

(Knowingly.)

He is.

RODIN

It is possible, perhaps even probable, as you assert, that he is wrong. However, it is also possible he is right.

(Short pause, while he is apparently thinking.)

But it occurs to me there is a third possibility we must consider. It could well be that he is pulling my leg.

MS. TIMID

(Trustingly.)

My mama's always right and she never tries to fool me so there must be a Santa.

RODIN

Nobody's *always* right.

THE BOY NEXT DOOR

(To Mr. Know-It-All.)

If there's no Santa Claus, who fills our stockings?

MR. KNOW-IT-ALL

Your dad and your mom, silly.

THE GIRL NEXT DOOR

How do *you* know?

MR. KNOW-IT-ALL

They gotta 'cause nobody could put toys in stockings of everyone in the whole world.

MS. TIMID

Santa can.

THE BOY NEXT DOOR

Yeah. His reindeer are real fast, like a cowboy's horse.

(He rides an imaginary horse around the stage.)

RODIN

(He holds up one hand to pause the conversation. One can see he is trying to calculate how fast Santa's sleigh would have to go.)

My dad says it takes a half a day to fly across the ocean. If that is true, Santa's reindeer would have to be faster than a jet!

MR. KNOW-IT-ALL

(Sure of himself.)

No reindeer could go that fast.

RODIN

I guess that's right.

(Raising his hand to give himself time again, seems to be speaking to himself.)

Could it be our parents are Santa's helpers?

MS. TIMID

Like the Santas with the bells.

(She holds her hand out, imitates a tired Salvation Army Santa Claus.)

THE BOY NEXT DOOR

Yeah.

MR. KNOW-IT-ALL

(Challengingly.)

If Santa's got lots of helpers filling the whole world's stockings, then what does he do?

MS. TIMID

Makes the toys with his elves.

MR. KNOW-IT-ALL

Then how come sometimes they're in boxes with prices like in the stores?

THE GIRL NEXT DOOR

Maybe Santa buys 'em there?

THE BOY NEXT DOOR

Or maybe Santa gives our mothers and fathers the money and they buy 'em. Just like my dad gives my mom money to buy stuff.

RODIN

If that were true, where would Santa get the money to give to our parents?

MR. KNOW-IT-ALL

Yeah.

MS. CYNIC

Who cares where he gets it? Maybe he just has it.

MS. TIMID

Maybe that’s what taxes are for.

THE BOY NEXT DOOR

I still think Santa brings the toys.

MR. KNOW-IT-ALL

(Cynically.)

In his sled?

RODIN

(In a tone of awe.)

Wow! It’d have to be a pretty big sled if everyone’s toys were in it!

MR. KNOW-IT-ALL

Yeah! An’ how would Santa fly through the air? (Makes motions of flying.) And get down a chimney? (Sinks to his knees as if going down a chimney.) Or get in a house without a chimney?

MS. TIMID

(Twirls around the stage, dancing like a wood nymph.)

Maybe he's magic, like fairies.

MS. CYNIC

(Shrugs.)

Who cares?

THE BOY NEXT DOOR

I bet his reindeer have wings!

MR. KNOW-IT-ALL

(Sticking out his tongue.)

Pooh!

THE GIRL NEXT DOOR

(Admonishing the boys, for she is frightened by all the heretic talk.)

You boys aren't going to get any presents if you don't believe in Santa.

THE BOY NEXT DOOR

(Hurriedly atoning for his sin.)

I've always believed in Santa!

MS. TIMID

So have I!

THE GIRL NEXT DOOR

Me too, 'cause he brings me presents.

RODIN

A question occurs to me. Why does Santa live at the North Pole?

MS. CYNIC

Who cares? Maybe he likes it there.

MS. TIMID

Maybe 'cause his house is there.

MR. KNOW-IT-ALL

'Cause he doesn't really live and nobody's seen his house so they think it must be way away away, like at the North Pole.

THE BOY NEXT DOOR

There must be a Santa Claus. I've always believed in him.

THE GIRL NEXT DOOR

There's gotta be 'cause I want him to bring me presents.

RODIN

Just because you want something doesn't mean you get it. Most things you want you will never get!

(Pause for laughter from the audience.)

MS. CYNIC

Most things you don't have, you want.

(Pause for more laughter from audience.)

THE GIRL NEXT DOOR

Why does Santa come on Christmas?

THE BOY NEXT DOOR

'Cause that's when he comes.

MS. TIMID

'Cause it's cold then, like at the North Pole?

MS. CYNIC

(Cynically.)

Maybe 'cause it's his birthday.

THE BOY NEXT DOOR

Maybe 'cause it says on the calendar he should come then.

RODIN

(With quiet assurance.)

You all know the answer. It's because

it's Jesus's (he carefully rolls a long series of s's to emphasize the possessive form of *Jesus*) birthday.

MR. KNOW-IT-ALL

Talk, talk. There's no Santa Claus.

MS. CYNIC

You talk, talk, talk. So what if there isn't or there is? If there is, there is. If not, not. So why talk? Talking doesn't change anything or make it real or unreal.

MR. KNOW-IT-ALL

We'll ask a grown-up.

(They look around for an adult).

There's one!

(They all run to where the playground fence should be, lean against it).

Mister. Mi-i-i-ster. Is there a Santa Claus?

MAN OFFSTAGE

Hello, children. Of course there is.

THE BOY NEXT DOOR, MS. TIMID, and THE GIRL NEXT DOOR

(All stick out tongues at Mr. Know-It-All)

Nyyaaa. We told you!

RODIN

You might wish to be careful. Do not jump to conclusions. One man's opinion does not create a truth.

THE BOY NEXT DOOR

Right.

(Points offstage.)

I want him to be right!

(Church bell tolls five times offstage.)

MS. TIMID

That's five o'clock, I have to go home.

THE GIRL NEXT DOOR

Me too. And I wanna be good 'cause Santa's coming.

MS. CYNIC

Who cares? Good schmud. Santa'll come or he won't.

(All three girls call good-bye as they run off.)

MR. KNOW-IT-ALL

(Bullying The Boy Next Door.)

You don't really believe, do ya?

THE BOY NEXT DOOR

(Bravely.)

'Course!

MR. KNOW-IT-ALL

An' how does Santa fly? An' get all those toys in his sled?

THE BOY NEXT DOOR

(Less brave.)

I dunno …

MR. KNOW-IT-ALL

(Brutally now.)

An' how come we've never seen a real Santa, only Santas with stuck-on beards? An' how does Santa remember what everyone wants, an' know how big to make their clothes? An' get down the chimney?

THE BOY NEXT DOOR

(Withering under the assault, turns to Rodin for support.)

How?

RODIN

(Cautiously.)

Maybe he's magic? But then again,

that's improbable. Dad says no magic is real.

MR. KNOW-IT-ALL

(Going in for the kill.)

An' how does Santa park his sled on a tilting roof? Or not forget even one anybody anywhere? Or know whatcha want an' never give ya something ya already got?

THE BOY NEXT DOOR

(Tears in his eyes, turns again to Rodin for support.)

You believe, dontcha?

RODIN

(Still speaking with that voice years beyond his age.)

I'm of two minds on this issue. There seems to be no real proof one way or the other.

MR. KNOW-IT-ALL

(Belligerent, bullying).

Kid stuff. You're a kid. Pooh! (Sarcastically.) Santa Claus!

THE BOY NEXT DOOR

(Crying now.)

But Mommy says there's a Santa Claus. I wanna Santa Claus!

MR. KNOW-IT-ALL

Just wantin' isn't goin' to help. Stupid, believing in Santa Claus.

THE BOY NEXT DOOR

(Sobbing.)

I'm goin' to tell my mommy on you.

WOMAN OFFSTAGE

Son … Son … We're going home.

THE BOY NEXT DOOR

That's my mommy. I'm going to ask my mommy.

MR. KNOW-IT-ALL

Kid stuff. Anyone knows there's no Santa.

WOMAN

(Comes on stage.)

There you are. We've got to go home, dear.

(Notices her son is crying.)

What's the matter, dear?

(Fearful they will be reprimanded, Mr. Know-It-All and Rodin hide behind the Christmas tree.)

THE BOY NEXT DOOR

(Sobbing.)

Some kids said there wasn't a Santa Claus.

WOMAN

(Embraces him.)

You mustn't believe everything you hear, sweetie. Of course there's a Santa Claus.

THE BOY NEXT DOOR

(Sobbing less, but not convinced.)

But how do his reindeer fly? An' how does he get down the chimney an' all?

WOMAN

He has special reindeer, and by putting his finger along his nose (she does this, showing how Santa does it) he goes down the chimney.

THE BOY NEXT DOOR

(Calming down.)

You're sure there's a Santa Claus?

WOMAN

Of course there is, dear.

THE BOY NEXT DOOR

How does he know what everyone wants, an' what size they wear, an' what color they like, an' what kind of candy they eat, an' how old they are, an' if they've been good or bad?

WOMAN

Santa Claus is very sweet and very, very wise.

(She pauses, searching for what to say, how she might convince her son.)

You know when we're in church, the pastor says God is love, that he loves everyone and knows everything about everyone. That's like Santa.

(She hugs her son.)

THE BOY NEXT DOOR

(Believing now, brightens and smiles.)

He knows everything about everyone! He loves everyone, gives everyone presents? He knows tomorrow is Christmas?

WOMAN

Yes, dear. Santa is very special.

(Mother and son start to walk offstage.)

THE BOY NEXT DOOR

I'm glad there's a Santa, Mommy. Believing in Santa Claus makes me happy. I don't understand how people can live without believing in Santa Claus!

(He smiles happily at his mother. She kneels down and gathers him in her arms.)

He knows everything about everyone! He knows what presents they want. He knows their favorite color and whether they've been good or bad. He loves everyone. I'm going to pray to him! I love Santa!

(They embrace joyfully. As the two leave the stage, he turns to the audience.)

Santa's like God! He loves everyone! He comes tomorrow! Merry Christmas! Merry Christmas!

(As The Boy Next Door and his mother leave the stage, the sound of the

Christmas carols swells. As soon as they exit, Mr. Know-It-All and Rodin come out from behind the tree. They stand for a moment looking offstage in the direction the mother and son went.)

MR. KNOW-IT-ALL

(He looks thoughtfully at the top of the tree and then turns to Rodin, speaking sarcastically.)

I'm glad he's happy. But his mom is wrong.

RODIN

(Still speaking like an adult.)

Well, let's consider. Perhaps she is right. Perhaps Santa *is* like God.

MR. KNOW-IT-ALL

No way!

(He puts his arm around Rodin's shoulder. The two of them walk slowly toward offstage. Rodin is still mulling over the question.)

RODIN

If Santa's like God, and the verb 'to be' is reflexive …

(Pause as he thinks about something his parents have told him about grammar, something he doesn't quite comprehend, so he repeats it with some importance.)

… is *reflexive*, then you can say it the other way.

MR. KNOW-IT-ALL

Reflexive?

RODIN

You know, like a mirror. If it's true one way, then it's true the other way.

MR. KNOW-IT-ALL

(Pause as he mulls that over.)

So saying Santa's like God is the same as saying God's like Santa?

RODIN

(Nods.)

I guess so.

(Speaks softly, to himself.)

If we can say Santa's like God, then we can also say God's like Santa.

(Stares at the top of the Christmas tree, thinking.)

Sounds funny when I say it that way, doesn't it?

(Mr. Know-It-All nods agreement as they again walk toward the exit.)

RODIN

(Again, more to himself than to his companion.)

It makes you think. When one says it backward, does it mean the same thing?

MR. KNOW-IT-ALL

(Shrugs. He's lost interest.)

All I know is there *is no Santa.*

(He exits.)

RODIN

(Demanding.)

Answer me! Is God like Santa Claus?

(The lights go out. As the curtain falls, Rodin cries out woefully, painfully in the darkness.)

Answer me. Is God like Santa?

LAST RITES

The stars glittered feebly as night died. In the distance, behind the ragged mountain peaks, a line of light presaged the dawn. It was that hour of transition between night and day, when the owls have ceased their hunting and the day birds have not yet begun to stir; when the stars are fading and the light of the rising sun has not yet seeped into the heavens. The world was black and still. The only sound came from the shuffle of feet on cobblestones as a crowd of men and women climbed through narrow, steep streets. The people were mourning the death of one of their most powerful priests and climbed toward their temple to witness primitive rites in commemoration of his passing. In the predawn darkness, they walked silently. This was a somber occasion.

The men of the crowd were clad much alike in short jackets, pants belted around their waists, and bits of cloth—like narrow bandannas—tied around their necks and hanging loosely down their chests. Their costumes were dyed somber hues of gray or black or brown, as prescribed by the solemn ritual. In contrast, the women were dressed in swaths of cloth dyed in bright pinks and yellows and reds. The focal point of their garb was the flowers, fruit, and bits of colorful cloth entwined in their hair, topped off by gaudy hats of various colors and sizes.

The town through which the crowd climbed clung to the steep hills that formed the northernmost tip of a peninsula that jutted between the sea to the west and a bay to the east. Inland, farther to the east, a mountain range towered magnificently. Since the bay served as a fine harbor, the town was a center of commerce. Trade and barter and moneylending flourished and attracted men from far-off lands. Some succeeded in finding the fortunes they sought; but most soon huddled with their kinfolk, forming enclaves where they spoke their own languages, carried on their own customs, and revered their own gods. In certain quarters, recent immigrants begged in the streets. Thus, this town, a city really, was well-known for its diversity of people and cultures. But it was particularly renowned for what its residents considered one of the most marvelous achievements of builders up to that time: a bridge that spanned the entrance of the harbor, allowing people to cross from the city to the villages to the north, and providing a short route for farmers so that they could carry their vegetables and wines to market. It was a bridge as large or larger than many previously built, and moreover was beautiful beyond words in the eyes of the people of this region.

But it was not the bridge the men and women thought about as they wound between the houses toward their temple. In the predawn darkness, they wrestled with the primitive emotions that had stirred hearts since the beginning of time: love and fear. For the minds of these people were fixed on the priest whom they mourned, and hence on their God. And though they loved their Divine One, these people also feared Him. They were like children whose drunkard father often plays with them, then suddenly and groundlessly kicks and cuffs them. They loved the Eternal Protector and yet they quaked on nearing His temple. Each dreaded approaching His altar. In them writhed the unvoiced fear that the All-Powerful One might strike them dumb, or blind, or might unleash His wrath on them in some horrible way. And yet to a man, these people would protest vehemently that they loved their God. And the irony is, they did.

It was still dark when the crowd reached the holy place and stealthily ascended the tier on tier of marble slabs that led to the gaping temple doors. Like a huge vulture perched on a heap of stones, the building hurtled ominously into the blackness above the worshippers. The structure was like this people's God: awe-inspiring and menacing. As the crowd drew into the shadow of the building, each person inwardly cringed, the women drawing their shawls tightly about them, for they were all too well aware of their special sins; and the men casting their eyes to the ground so as not to appear too proud. Like fearful dogs, the people crept into the blackness of their temple.

Inside was all darkness. The ceiling was flung so high that it could not be seen, and the rough-hewn stone walls were frightening, towering shadows. Flickering tapers endeavored to light the ominous void, but they were feeble pinpoints of light that fluttered and wavered and threatened to blow out at any moment. At the front of the temple, two young boys, obviously in apprenticeship for the priesthood, edged warily up to a monolith, the great stone block that served as an altar, and with trembling fingers lit the tapers arranged around it. When all the tapers were lit, the boys backed fearfully away from the altar, then crouched in obeisance to the Divine One, as if begging His pardon for approaching so near to this most sacred of stones.

The tapers flickered eerily in the darkness, illuminating the massive altar and glimmering on the single shaft of metal that sprang vertically from it before blossoming into three prongs of equal length. About the altar, a knee-high fence kept the worshippers from drawing too near to the hallowed rock and possibly incurring the Divine One's fury, but it was superfluous. The worshippers would not have dared venture near to the altar with its three-pronged metal shaft.

The worshippers were utterly silent, and yet the silence deepened as the gigantic doors to the temple swung shut. Tiny bells sounded, and the hushed congregation rose to its feet. Then, from the darkness under the eaves, the silence was shattered by myriad voices swelling joyfully in songs of praise. The voices soared and danced, alternately leaping to mountain peaks and wandering in valley depths, singing praises to the Most Wondrous One. And then the voices rose like a giant wave bearing down on a beach until they broke in an ecstatic crescendo, and at that moment the priests swept into the temple in splendid procession. They were robed in vestments of fine silks dyed various hues and embroidered with religious symbols. They carried sacred charms, and from the procession the sweet aroma of incense diffused through the dank air. As they marched at a stately pace, they chanted incantations designed to please the Divine One, so He would look upon both them and the rest of the people with favor. It was an impressive display of beauty and veneration, and the people could not help but feel that these rituals pleased their God.

When the priests had ranged themselves about the altar,

the head priest began chanting prayers in a language reserved solely for the temple. At times he chanted alone, his voice lifting mystically, musically, almost singing the strange language; and at times the other priests either joined him or responded to him. Even the main body of worshippers often joined in. Although they could not understand the language, they had often heard the prayers and knew that this one described the Divine One's might, that one was an entreaty to Him to be merciful, that a third honored his benevolence; and on certain cues they murmured incantations taught them by the priests. During this chanting, the head priest and one or two of the sub-priests performed certain movements and gestures before the altar that they knew caused the Divine One to smile favorably upon the rituals. Every motion and gesture, each word of every prayer, was made in strict accordance with the ancient traditions of the religion. The priests did not dare to venture outside the code that had been handed down to them through the centuries. There was no telling what evil might befall them if they were so bold.

These initial rites continued for some time, for the Divine One had to be flattered and extoled to ensure that He would provide bountiful harvests and substantial profits and would keep other tribes from attacking the city and the nation. More songs of praise rang from under the rafters, and more incense was burned until, finally, the priests deemed that the core of the rituals could begin.

With reverence, the head priest placed on the altar a metal vessel wrought with efficacious symbols. From the delicate manner in which he handled the vessel and from its intricate design, this obviously was a bowl of great value. Moreover, its contents were priceless. The bowl contained a small amount of the blood of the deceased priest whom the people mourned.

A penetrating silence fell over the worshippers and the priest as the vessel on the altar captured their attention. In the light of the flickering tapers, it glimmered with a surprising brilliance. In the eyes of the people, it emanated a supernatural radiance. The death of their great priest had sorrowed these worshippers; and though they well knew he had died, at the sight of the bowl containing his blood, his presence seemed to creep about them in the darkness. In this eerie setting, they could easily imagine what the priests had told them, that the dead man had in some mysterious way taken on various of the attributes of the Divine One and henceforth would lurk in the darkness of the temple. Not only did the presence of this deceased priest permeate the darkness at this most sacred moment, the spirits of other dead men seemed to swirl about the worshippers. The head priest had reminded them in prayers of other priests who had died after living lives of great glory, and he had pleaded earnestly to the memories of those dead men, begging them to persuade the Divine One to be merciful. To assure that these supplications succeeded, the priests had hidden under the altar remnants of some of these long-dead men, bits of bone and shreds of their clothing, for it seemed obvious such relics would be effective charms.

Near the bowl of blood on the altar, the head priest placed pieces cut from the body of the dead man in a matching bowl, and in the absolute silence of the temple he whispered further entreaties to the Divine One and to the dead priest. Carefully, exactly, he continued through a series of rituals and prayers, every gesture of which was of utmost significance. Often, he traced the shape of the vertical metal shaft with its three prongs, for this was known to be an especially effective symbol. And often during this most holy of rites, the tiny bells were rung to emphasize the importance of a certain prayer or movement.

Satisfied that these rituals had been properly completed, the head priest approached the vessels on the altar. He moved slowly, silently, solemnly, and from the worshippers there came no sound. Everyone was enshrouded in the mystery, the reverence, of the moment. As if in slow motion, the priest raised the first bowl into the air, and a thousand eyes fixed on the gleaming metal as if in hopes of seeing the spirit of the great priest appear above it like a phantom. Then the priest lowered the bowl, brought it to his lips, and drank some of the blood. Ceremonially, he swallowed a bit of the dead man's body, then passed the vessels to the remaining priests, who imitated him. The meaning behind the primitive ceremony was obvious to these people: by drinking his blood and devouring his flesh, a person shared in the pain and sorrow of the priest's death, while simultaneously acquiring some of his divinity and glory.

After the priests had consumed their share of the vessels' contents, it was the worshippers' turn. Apprehensively, they formed a line and shuffled to the front of the temple, where they received a morsel of the dead man's body and a sip of his blood. Although most of these worshippers had experienced fear simply on entering the temple, the fear they experienced in partaking in this grisly act of cannibalism was a hundredfold greater. Thus, it was not surprising that on returning to their places, their expressions were as though they were in a trance. The tension, the fear, and the elaborate proceedings were needed for these primitive rites to succeed. These people would swear evermore that they had felt the power and the glory of the great priest flow through them when they consumed his flesh and blood.

Now that this central portion of the service was completed, the patience of the city's people was worn. They waited restlessly while the head priest performed the last portions of the rites; and he, sensing the worshippers' impatience, hurried through the remaining prayers. The windows of the temple were already aflame with many colors: reds, blues, and violets splashed in patches over the congregation. Dawn was slipping over the land, and the people wanted to escape the gloom of the rough stone building. Religion provided their lives with a necessary dimension, but they did not want this dimension to interfere with their workaday world.

When the priests had completed the last ritual, the congregation swarmed from the benches toward the now open doors. In the crush toward the light and fresh air, people hailed friends and acquaintances, chatted and exchanged bits of gossip, their God and their fear forgotten, discarded in the dark recesses of the stone building.

Outside on the steps, two men paused to exchange a few words of greeting. They spoke of the weather, as men of every epoch have done. The first, a moneylender, had made a loan to his friend some weeks before. The friend was a farmer who had used the loan for fertilizer. Each of them hoped the fine weather would hold. A good crop of grapes from the vast vineyards of the region would make them both rich.

Laughing and talking, they looked out across the city, enjoying the fine view. To the east, the harbor sparkled brightly; farther east, inland, snow glistened in the mountains; and to the west, the ocean stretched infinitely. Traffic was already clogging the steep streets, creeping across the marvelous bridge for which the city was so famous.

The two men slapped each other on the back. Together they descended the steps to the street, where they went their separate ways. Behind them, the stone tower reared ominously above the marble steps, but the two men were out of its shadow, in the press of the crowds on the street, and their thoughts slid away from their God. As the farmer started down the steep slope, he stopped for a last glimpse of the bridge spanning the entrance to the harbor, golden in the early morning light, and he marveled, as he always did, at its beauty. As he watched, the sun rose higher, and its rays touched on the ruins of a building on a small island in the bay. Previously, the farmer knew, the building and the island had served as a prison. More recently, the complex had become a magnet for tourists. Beyond the island, the bay sparkled brilliantly, and the snow on the rocky peaks of the mountain range shimmered pink in the rays of the rising sun. The farmer put the death of the powerful priest behind him. It was the dawn of a new and glorious day. On Monday, after the holiday weekend was over, he would return to his vineyards in Sonoma. With luck, it would be a good year for grapes and for the wine they would yield.

THE MAHARAJAH AND THE DEVIL

It was a strange game. On one side of the table the Maharajah, intense, absorbed, oblivious. Across from him the wayfarer, enjoying his wine and flirting with the women of his host's harem. The Maharajah was renowned as the richest man in India and the best poker player in all the East. Hardly a fortnight elapsed without two or three strangers arriving at his castle wishing to gamble with him—and never did he refuse. This wayfarer, playing so casually, was such a one. But he was unique. He was winning.

It was the wayfarer's deal. The cards whirred like a hummingbird's wing as he shuffled. His hands flashed as he dealt: five cards appeared instantly before both the Maharajah and him. While the Maharajah considered his hand, the wayfaring stranger captured the wrist of a brown-skinned girl hovering nearby—she was one of the harem—and teased her for a good-luck kiss. The Maharajah placed his bet. The stranger carelessly matched the bet, his cards lying untouched before him.

"Two," the Maharajah said. He was drawing to a pair of nines and a king. The stranger's fingers flashed, and two cards lay before the host. Glancing now at his own hand, the wayfarer indicated he would draw none.

The Maharajah bet. Still teasing the brown-skinned girl, the stranger raised. The host pondered. He had drawn a king; he now held two pairs, kings and nines. He decided to raise again. Laughing, the wayfarer raised once more. The Maharajah called.

"For luck," joked the stranger, and the girl kissed him lightly. "Two pairs," he announced. "Kings."

"And what?" asked the Maharajah.

"Fours."

"And nines." The Maharajah smiled, revealing two kings and two nines as he swept the pot toward him. The stacks of coins on either side of the table were now roughly equal. The stranger shrugged, teasing as he accused the brown-skinned girl of causing his bad luck.

At that moment, a servant slipped into the hall, bowed, and announced that dinner was prepared. If his lordship so desired ... The Maharajah did. He invited the wayfarer to join him, and in the best of spirits the two entered the banquet hall to partake of the sumptuous evening meal. The fare was royal: roast duck and pheasant, wine and champagne, and bowls heaped with an array of fruits. The wayfarer ate hugely and drank copiously. He obviously enjoyed the meal, as well as the girls and the Maharajah's company. As for the Maharajah, he was in rare high spirits.

He explained to the stranger that it had been a long time since he had enjoyed a game of poker as much as that night. Ever since his wife had died, while she bore the son who would have been his heir, poker had been his only amusement. But for the last few years, this pastime had been devoid of pleasure. For, the Maharajah explained, he never lost. It was not that he never played any experts, it was merely that his opponents' funds were always limited, and his were limitless. As any card player knows, the gambler who has unlimited funds can never lose.

"To always win!" the stranger said, smirking. "It hardly sounds like an unhappy fate."

The Maharajah sighed. "But it is. And with no wife, with no son, and with my only pleasure shriveling like a raisin, it is indeed a sorry existence that I now lead." Pensive, the Maharajah sipped his cognac. "But." He suddenly smiled. "Tonight you have changed all that. You play brilliantly!"

"I thank you." The stranger grinned, revealing sharp white teeth. "I also compliment you on your game. You were my equal. This evening. But …" His grin shifted to a diabolical leer. "But I warn you, at gambling I have no equal. Not if I desire to win."

The Maharajah raised his eyebrows skeptically.

"Tonight's game was unimportant," the stranger said. "We played for money. You are so rich that money means nothing to you. And to me, money is only what buys men. So, the game was a farce. The stakes meant nothing to either of us."

As the stranger spoke, the Maharajah noticed a change come over him. Whereas the stranger's attention had been casual and unfocused so far that night, his eyes now burned with an inward desire. The man seemed aflame with a passion, his eyes glimmering like the eyes of a wild boar charging to kill.

"You do not believe me," he said. "I tell you, poker is a farce, a sham, a mockery as we played it tonight. Poker, real poker, must be played for stakes that are priceless. It is only when a man gambles what he dare not lose, what he cannot lose, that poker is as it is meant to be."

The Maharajah laughed. "No man gambles what he

cannot lose. Perhaps a man gambles a year's wages, two years' wages, and yet, even to a poor man, that is not everything. What a man dare not lose, he will not gamble."

The stranger's eyes narrowed. He leaned forward. The light painted his intense features a reddish hue. "You are right. Few men dare to gamble what they cannot lose. And it is only those few men who know poker as it should be played."

Still leaning forward, the stranger sipped the last of the cognac in his snifter. The glass, just as his face, glowed crimson. The Maharajah could have sworn that the cognac had turned to molten fire.

"Would not you," the stranger asked, "want to gamble what you dare not lose?"

A smile crept across the Maharajah's face as he divined this gambler's purpose. "I am not such a fool," he replied. "I do not know what you want from me, but I would not stake at cards what I dared not lose."

"Perhaps." The stranger grinned wickedly. "I believe I could convince you. Would you like a son?"

The Maharajah laughed heartily. "For a son, I could be convinced to stake my kingdom, my castle, yes, the whole of my kingdom and castle and everything therein! Everything. But an heir has been denied me these many years. And now …" He stroked his beard, and his eyes twinkled. "I do believe it is too late."

"Not so," replied the guest. "Do you see that girl?" He pointed to the girl he had teased earlier in the evening. "Take her to be the Maharani, your wife, and within the year she will bear you a son."

"Me? A son? You are a fool."

"Perhaps. And perhaps not. But let me finish. In exchange for this son, you must promise to play one hand of poker with me. The stakes, those you just proposed: your kingdom and everything therein. Do you agree?"

The Maharajah laughed till he spilled his cognac. Sarcastically, he asked, "And this one hand of poker will thus be poker as it should be played?"

"Precisely." Again, the stranger leaned forward intently, as if hypnotizing his host.

"Who do you think you are," the Maharajah asked, still amused, "that you can promise me a son? Brahma?"

As the Maharajah made the joke, he went suddenly ashen. He stared at the stranger's face. The eyes! They were not the eyes of a mortal. And the shape of the face! The elongated, almost pointed chin and diamond-shaped ears. As the Maharajah stared, a sardonic smile flickered over the wayfarer's face, and the Maharajah became aware of the eyes burning with the wickedness of another world. The room grew suddenly hot, so hot that the Maharajah thought the walls must be aflame, and the air seemed to reverberate with the screams of tortured men.

The stranger smiled. "I see you recognize me."

"Satan!" murmured the Maharajah, dumbfounded. "Satan himself."

"Yes. Are you still doubtful about the son?" The Maharajah did not answer. "Well?" said the guest. "Do you agree to my proposal? A son for a hand of cards?"

The Maharajah was still more amused than convinced at the idea of begetting a son; and amused that Satan would think that he, the Maharajah, would stumble into a trap, whatever trap that might be, by ceding blindly to temptation. The temptation so blatantly dangled by the Devil himself was a jest, not a matter of serious consideration. And yet ... The Maharajah felt himself sliding toward sin. Felt himself wanting to act on emotion, to say yes, willing to bargain with Satan.

He reined himself in. “I need to ponder the matter,” he said finally. “Give me some time.” And then, more to himself than to Satan, he murmured, “A son. The son I have always dreamed of. But losing my kingdom?” He wondered, shaking his head, if Satan could do as he boasted.

Satan snickered. “I perceive a note of hesitancy. Is it, perhaps, that you do not trust me?”

“History…” began the Maharajah.

Satan laughed outright. “I am not asking you to trust me. But consider the matter. I will receive your answer in the morning.”

He stood and bowed politely, and the Maharajah beckoned to one of the attendants, ordering him to show the guest to his quarters.

“Good night,” the Maharajah said politely. “My servants will do your bidding.”

“As most people do,” Satan answered. “Good night, your Highness. And consider the matter carefully.”

The two bowed in parting, and they did not meet again until they had slept and breakfasted. Or rather, until Satan had slept and breakfasted, for the Maharajah was haggard after a night of pacing the floor.

“Your decision?” asked Satan, who seemed in a fine humor.

“I have given the matter much thought,” the Maharajah replied. “I accept, with two conditions. First, we limit the stakes. I will stake my kingdom and everything in it, as you ask, but not the castle itself.” He smiled wryly. “In the event I lose, I will need a place to sleep.”

Satan nodded. “Agreed. It would not be in my character,” he added with amusement, “to be excessively greedy. Let us say that we limit our wager to the kingdom and everything in it, excepting the castle."

"The second condition: the son you promise me must be born healthy and normal."

"Rest assured. He will have as much capacity for sin as others." More seriously, he added, "I promise the boy will be born normal."

The two men mused for a moment, considering their wager. After the moment passed, the Maharajah asked, "How do we proceed from here?"

"In one year precisely, your son will be born. Three years from today, I will return. At that time, your son will be two years old. We will play one hand of five card stud. If you win, you will have your kingdom free and clear. If I win, your kingdom and everything in it, excepting the castle, is mine." He smiled, adding grandly, "I suspect that if I to win, I could be convinced to be uncharacteristically generous"—he paused and smirked—"and leave you a small stipend to support you and your castle in your old age. In the meantime, you and the Maharani," he added with a nod at the brown-skinned girl, "will become parents of a healthy boy a year from today. Agreed?"

"Agreed," replied the Maharajah, and the two of them bowed to seal the bargain.

"Until three years from today," Satan said. "Au revoir."

Before the Maharajah could reconsider, Satan vanished, leaving a swirl of red dust where he had stood.

Now, the Maharajah was no fool. He was convinced Satan would try to fix the outcome of their poker game, yet a kernel of hope persisted in him. Might he not be able to defeat Satan? Find a way to defeat him? To trick him perhaps? So his thoughts ran. And, he consoled himself, at the worst, he would be stripped of his power and his wealth, but he would have gained a son and would still have his castle. With luck, he might find a way to save his kingdom. Though how? he wondered. He mulled the question time and again, but as the months went by, and his new wife swelled with child, he forgot Satan and turned his mind to joyful anticipation of the birth of his son. What Satan wanted was not important. He was soon to have an heir.

Twelve months to the day after the Devil's visit, the monarch's son was born. He was a lusty, robust child, and the Maharajah could hardly believe his good fortune. He had a son! An heir! It was inconceivable, so inconceivable that the Maharajah felt the need to verify his son's existence countless times each day. Hence, he could be seen traipsing to the nursery at odd hours of the day or night in order to catch a glimpse of the babe.

The boy grew quickly, and in no time at all—or so it seemed to his father—he was crawling, then standing, then repeating simple words and nearly walking. Everyone said, and it was true, the boy was the spitting image of his father. The Maharajah was delighted with the child's progress, and wishing to educate him well, he inquired after able tutors. The child was too young to begin his formal education, the Maharajah knew, but it was not too early to begin planning that education. Especially when the lad was as able as this youngster!

In no time at all, it was the child's first birthday, and the monarch declared it to be a day of celebration for all his people. A great party was held on the grounds outside the castle, with roasted pig and jugs of wine and much dancing and singing. The Maharaja himself carried his son through the throngs of his subjects, the proud father pointing out the qualities of the youngster to the admiration of all.

Now that he was one year old, it was time to begin the education of the prince. The tutor who had been selected began the boy's tutelage. In no time at all, it seemed, the tutor was asking the Maharajah about the required course of study for the child's second year. The question jolted the Maharajah. In a few weeks' time, the boy would be two! He and the Maharani would be celebrating their third anniversary. The three years since the Devil's last visit were about to elapse. Satan would return. The unease that had gnawed at the Maharajah when he first made his pact with the Devil welled in him again. How could he beat Satan? Was there any way he could save his kingdom?

During the weeks remaining before Satan's return, the Maharajah diligently prepared for the eventuality of the loss of his kingdom. He set the financial matters of the realm in order and resolved all unsettled controversies between his people. He designated his most trusted advisor to be ruler once he, the Maharajah, was forced to step down, and prepared the man for his coming responsibilities. Thus readied, the Maharajah awaited the fateful day. He was not overjoyed at the thought of the Satanic visit, but considered, even should he lose his realm, the bargain had been a good one. He had become entranced by the laughter and joy of his heir, the young prince. His son, his heir, was well worth the price of his kingdom, if it came to that.

Then came the day of Satan's return. The Maharajah spent the morning in the nursery watching his son play, listening to him recite his few simple words and phrases. What a smiling, happy, healthy lad he was! It would make old age easy to bear, to watch his son grow and mature and carry on family traditions.

At that moment, a servant entered to announce that a stranger at the gate, dressed all in red, declared he had an appointment with the Maharajah. Was he to be shown in? The monarch nodded. Yes.

The Maharajah greeted Satan, and after exchanging formalities, the host suggested they dine together before getting to the business at hand.

"A wonderful idea," replied the Devil, who seemed in the best of spirits. "The meal you served on my last visit was superb. You recall my visit?" The Maharajah nodded. "Good." Satan laughed. "It can be so unpleasant when a person forgets and I am forced to refresh their memory. But we will discuss our bargain after dinner."

As before, the meal the Maharajah served was regal. Deer heart and liver, wild peacock and a roast suckling pig cooked to a golden brown. Each course was accompanied by its own well-aged wine and carried in on platters heaped artistically with vegetables and fruits.

"Truly delicious." Satan sighed contentedly after having gorged himself. "I often wonder at how easy it is to convince mortals that life is intolerable."

"Do you find it easy?" the Maharajah asked. "I always assumed it took rather a lot of work on your part."

"To the contrary. It's child's play. I simply focus the subject's attention on the unfortunate but inescapable aspects of life—sickness, old age, death—and poof! Most men turn bitter in an instant."

"You believe men are unable to accept sickness, old age, and death? But you must agree those concepts are hard to understand if one wishes to believe that life is all good?"

"Perhaps," answered Satan, sipping from his snifter. "But it always seemed obvious to me that life cannot exist without decay and death. What is life, after all?"

He leaned back, pausing as he appreciatively sipped the last of the liquor from his glass, and then answered his own question.

"Life is motion, and motion presupposes direction. Life's direction is decay, death. Eliminate decay and death, you eliminate life's direction, and hence its motion. That is, you eliminate life itself. So, sickness, old age, and death are perhaps unfortunate consequences of life, but they are inescapable."

Smiling at his host, Satan continued. "You have been aware of that for many years. It is why you have not seen more of me. I know I cannot sour you. You accept life—accept death."

He looked questioningly at his host. "Do you agree with my definition of life?"

The Maharajah poured himself and his guest another snifter of cognac. He savored the bouquet of the amber liquid as he considered the question.

"I cannot disagree," he firmly replied, "but whereas you define life rather scientifically, I have always viewed it more aesthetically. To me, life is composed of three factors: creation, appreciation, and love. If a man does not create, if he does not appreciate his environment, and if he does not love, then he does not live. He is dead." The Maharajah smiled at his guest. "I know you agree. I have seen much of your handiwork. You have killed many men. You have caused them to cease being creative, caused them to cease appreciating their environment, and caused them to curl inwards, to cease loving."

Satan nodded. "Yes, you are right." A faraway look came into his eyes as he seemed to recall the many men he had corrupted. "I remember one man ..." he started gleefully, then broke off. “But that story wouldn’t interest you.” He stopped as if preparing for a new topic of conversation. “Your son,” he began. “He pleases you?”

The Maharajah glowed at the question. “A remarkable child. Most remarkable. Would you like to see him?” Proud father that he was, he did not wait for a reply, but ordered one of his servants to have the child brought in.

When the servant returned, the Maharajah smiled broadly at the sight of his son. “A remarkable child,” he exclaimed. “Destined for a grand future. Note the light in his eyes,” he boasted. “Already it is clear he is truly gifted.”

The lad’s eyes focused on his father, and his face lit up with the quick and pure pleasure revealed only in a young child’s mien. With one hand he reached toward the Maharajah, who extended a finger for the child to grasp. As the two of them played, it was clear that strong bonds of affection joined them.

“A healthy, spirited creature,” agreed Satan, as though he were speaking of a dog or judging a thoroughbred horse. Then, looking at the Maharajah, he asked, “What do you see in his future?”

“His future is his own to determine,” the Maharajah replied simply. “It will be enough for me if he lives, not as you define living, but as I define it.”

Satan grinned. “Growing old is not good enough?”

The Maharajah shook his head. “Certainly not. The living dead is your kind. The living are bound to create, appreciate, and love. But within that framework, my son is free to choose his own life.”

With that, Satan roared with laughter. “Free to choose! I’ve always liked that expression. Free choice is what keeps me in business.” Throwing his head back, Satan howled at his own joke.

The Maharajah did not join in the Devil's mirth, but returned the child to the servant, who carried him from the room. With the child gone, silence fell between the host and his guest. Satan's laughter had reminded the Maharajah of the choice he had made three years before —and for which he now had to pay. As the silence deepened, he shifted nervously in his chair. Finally, Satan smiled, though it was more a leer than a smile, and cleared his throat.

"Shall we get to the matter at hand?"

Reluctantly, the Maharajah rose. Gesturing toward the next room, he invited his guest to join him. "The cards await us."

Host and guest passed into the next room and took their places at the poker table. On the table stood a bottle of cognac and two snifters, and beside them a deck of cards. The Maharajah poured the drinks, the two men lifted their glasses, toasted each other, and drank.

Satan nodded with satisfaction, took a second sip. "Oh, my. Formidable!" He pronounced *formidable* with a thick French accent.

After a few minutes of silence as the two men enjoyed the cognac, the Maharajah slid the cards toward Satan to be shuffled. Magnanimously, Satan indicated that his host should shuffle, and then smiled at his own display of generosity. Neither of the two players spoke as the Maharajah performed the task, and the whirring of the cards echoed loudly in the chamber. Spreading the cards, the Maharajah selected one, as did Satan. The Devil turned up the jack of spades, the Maharajah the queen of hearts. It was the Maharajah's deal.

Coolly, the Maharajah handled the cards. He had

expected that he would be nervous, that the game would frighten him, but he found that this was not the case. He had prepared himself well these past weeks, convincing himself that his kingdom was a fair exchange for the son he had been given. He was resigned to losing and found even that a good bargain. And if he should win … That would simply be extra good fortune.

Looking up from the cards he shuffled, the Maharajah observed that Satan was studying him. A smile flickered on the Devil's face, the smile of one who knows he has the upper hand. For an instant, fear choked the Maharajah, but the fear passed as he reminded himself that he could at worst lose his kingdom, and he had already prepared himself for that. Yet those eyes … they promised a worse fate.

Politely, the Devil said, "Three years ago I assured you that our game today would be unlike any other poker you have played. That this would be real poker."

"And real poker," the Maharajah said, "is poker played for stakes which a man dare not lose. Correct?"

"Exactly."

Inwardly, the Maharajah smiled. "Then your assurance was for naught."

"Oh?" Satan said, and two flames flickered wickedly in his eyes. "There is nothing you dare not lose?"

The sight of those eyes, Satan's assurance of victory, again caused the fear to jump in the Maharajah's throat, but only for a moment.

"Nothing," he pronounced flatly. "There is nothing I dare not lose."

"I see." Satan smiled, and behind his eyes, the flames burned happily. "But it is my experience that every man values something that he dare not lose. Not so?"

"His kingdom, you mean?"

"Yes and no. You, I know, value your kingdom. Most men would. History shows that kingdoms are often of more value to a monarch than the monarch's own life." He chuckled. "I have lost track of how many hundreds of wars I have instigated, tempting a king to fight, to risk his own life, to spill the blood of thousands, only to die on the battlefield in unadulterated selfishness to preserve his power. Yes, to many men, their life is paramount, but the most powerful are wont to place their fiefdoms ahead of their own lives. But for good or bad—and I much prefer when it is for *bad* …" He paused, and his tongue flicked like the tongue of a snake, caressing his lips as if savoring the word *bad*. "Where was I? I lose my train of thought at the taste of sin." He collected himself. "Oh, yes. Sometimes there is an object, a principle, though more often a sin"—he again seemed to savor the word *sin* —"that, for good or bad, a man holds dearer even than his life."

At that, Satan paused and leaned forward. To the Maharajah, Satan was coiling like a snake ready to strike, his tongue darting in and out between his teeth. As had happened three years before, the room grew suddenly hot, so hot that the Maharajah thought the walls must be aflame, and the air seemed to reverberate with the screams of tortured men.

"Before you deal," Satan whispered, "we must clarify the terms of our wager."

The Maharajah's brows lifted. "The terms are clear. My kingdom."

Satan laughed. "It is as it always is. Mortals always underestimate me. Underestimate my ability to wreak havoc."

The Maharajah protested, battling back his rising fear. “You gave your word. Our wager was to be my kingdom, less the castle.”

“Almost precise.” Another broad smile as the Devil raised his arms in a magnanimous gesture. “But I have changed my mind. You may keep your kingdom.” He watched with seeming glee as the Maharajah released a sigh of relief. “Yes, you may keep your kingdom, but for—” He stopped in midsentence. “Remember the wager precisely. Remember, your stake was to be your kingdom. Your kingdom and everything in it.” A short pause. “Yes,” and now he spoke slowly, with emphasis, repeating “and everything in it.” He paused again, and with a wicked smile, continued. “But I will be magnanimous. You may keep your kingdom. All we will wager is that one object in your kingdom which you prize above all else. That which you prize more than your own life. For only then will we be playing poker as it should be played.”

“Dearer than my life,” the Maharajah mouthed softly, considering what it was he owned that might be dearer to him than his life. “Dearer than my life. No.” He shook his head. “You are mistaken. There is nothing I hold dearer than m—” His voice caught in his throat, and a sudden spasm shook him. The skin of his face blanched, and the pupils of his eyes dilated in fear. His hands trembled as do the hands of an old, old man.

“No!” he gasped, and another spasm shook him. “No, no, no.” He covered his face with his hands.

A smile flickered and danced on the Devil’s face. “Yes,” Satan said. “Your son.”

The room shook with the berserk laughter of hundreds of men in a madhouse. Satan’s pointed teeth morphed into fangs. His eyes blazed fanatically, like a crazed lioness tearing at the throat of a gazelle, tasting the hot blood pumping from the still-fluttering heart.

"Yes," he said again, and licked his lips "Yes, it is your son you dare not lose. It is your son you prize above all else, above your kingdom, above even your own life. Yes, it is your son whom we will wager."

"No," the Maharajah murmured, and again, "No … no … I was prepared to give my jewels, my kingdom, my castle, my life. But I should have known … should have guessed …"

His body heaved pitifully in great sobs, and he hid his face in his hands in an attempt to conceal the agony in his eyes. Finally, the wretched man looked up, uncovering his face, and anyone present would have sworn this was not the man who had dined with the Devil just minutes before. The mouth was distorted with grief, the eyes spread wide in pain, and the skin of his face hung dead over the bones of his cheeks. Even the beard and hair seemed whiter, sparser, than before. In a flicker, in no more than a spasm of time, the Maharajah had aged years.

"If you win," he said, his voice heavy with hurt, "what will you do to my son? Kill him?"

Satan smiled broadly. The Maharajah's sorrow was fuel for the flames that danced ecstatically behind his eyes. "Kill him? No, that I cannot do. Not even I"—and he emphasized the *I*—"have the power to kill." His tone settled. It quieted to that of a businessman laying out the terms of a contract. "No, I cannot kill." With a sly smile, he continued. "Nor would that please me. It is far more satisfying, far more amusing, to watch as a man ruins himself. Amusing to watch a sane man make a series of conscious decisions, decisions that inexorably lead to his own ruin, even his death." He paused, seeming to savor a delectable morsel. "Ahh, sin is delicious."

As the Maharajah watched, Satan picked up the cognac bottle and offered some to his host, who refused with a shake of his head. Satan poured himself a glass, admired the clarity of the amber fluid, sniffed its aroma, and sipped with obvious, somewhat exaggerated pleasure.

"Delicious." A broad smile for the Maharajah. "You do know your cognac. But …" He paused, as if searching for words. "Nothing, not this cognac, not the finest wine or most succulent meat can match the taste of sin."

His tongue flicked across his lips, tasting, enjoying an inner pleasure. That flick of the tongue caused the Maharajah to shudder. He had come to notice it as one of the Devil's tics, and once he had noticed it, it seemed that Satan licked his lips almost continuously.

"Most good tastes," Satan went on, "affect the lips and the tongue. Sin is tasted there as well. And it is truly delicious. But sin is more than a delicious taste. Sin is visceral. It satisfies deep within me."

Abruptly, he turned away from describing the taste of sin, as if the discussion was revealing too much of himself.

"Where were we? No, I cannot kill a man. But a man can be encouraged, can't he?" A broad smile. "I cannot kill, perhaps, but I can tempt." Another flick of the tongue and a bit of a leer. *Tempt*, the Maharajah realized, was another word with a specially delicious flavor for his tormentor. "Tempt. Cajole. Influence," the Devil continued. "I believe you know that history has proven that I am rather good in the sphere of creating desire."

Another sip of cognac, and again that flick of the tongue over his lips. Satan tilted his head, seeming to look through the ceiling to the clouds above. Musing, almost to himself, he said, "Remember our earlier meeting? We were discussing the future of your son, the one you doubted you would beget. Free to choose, you said. He would be free to choose." He smiled, toying with the Maharajah. "Free choice. I love it! What a concept. Free choice on the one hand, sin on the other. A pair made in heaven." He laughed at his joke.

Facing each other across the table, the Devil and the Maharajah sat. Silence for a bit, and then, hesitantly, fearfully, the Maharajah asked, "What do you have in store for my son? What is your plan for him? If *you* cannot kill him, what then? An accident? Or is it suicide?"

"I have confirmed that *I* cannot kill him. But I suppose it is not beyond the realm of possibility that I can influence him in this regard." He wagged a finger at the Maharajah. "An accident? No. One must be more gracious. Remember the two words I love? Free choice." He smiled, again licking his lips. "I do not wish to impose. I prefer to let a man select his own downfall. But you choose such a harsh word for his demise. Suicide is a despicable word. Let us avoid that word. Perhaps we should say that my plan for your son is to withdraw from the realm of the living. Isn't that more gently put?"

"In what manner?" the Maharajah cried out in torment. "How will you drive him to suicide?"

"Ahhh." Satan laughed. "I have told you already. Men have only to be made aware of sickness, old age, and death in order to do my bidding. If I win our little game" —Satan nodded at the cards and grinned, as if assured of victory— "then I have won the right to appear four times before your son. With four appearances, I will convince your son to, ahhh …" Satan hesitated, searching for the right word. "To … ahhh … No, let's not use the word 'suicide,' such a brutal word…." He seemed to be talking to himself rather than to the Maharajah. "No, not 'suicide.' Let's say we let him decide to quit the realm of the living." He smiled at his choice of words.

A low moan escaped the lips of the Maharajah before he shouted, "Kill himself! You will not make my son commit suicide. You cannot." He was suddenly broken and old, his vehemence spent, and he cradled his face in his quivering hands. "No … no … no …"

"Of course," Satan said, cackling as if he were telling a good joke, "you still have a chance. All you have to do is win at poker."

In spite of Satan's obvious sarcasm, the possibility of averting his son's doom revived the monarch somewhat. With an effort, he pulled himself together, wiped the tears from his eyes, and once again riffled the cards. But whereas his hands had been deft and sure a few minutes before, now they shook and fumbled; he could hardly hold the pack.

"What is the matter, my good man?" Satan asked. "Could it be that you fear losing? And so recently, it was that you complained of always winning!"

The Maharajah did not answer the Devil, but stared wildly at one corner of the hall. His son had suddenly appeared there! The lad screamed mightily, as though a sword had pierced his belly, and then it was clear why. Four figures were gathered in the far corner of the room, four shadowy, indistinct forms. The first of them glided silently toward the toddler, who screamed again at the apparition. And well he might, for the figure was ugly beyond belief, a wizened skeleton of a man bent almost double under a lumped, humped back. Flesh rotted with a putrid stench around putrescent wounds on the man's side, and flies swarmed over his face, crawling in and out of eye sockets that gaped horribly, black holes where the eyeballs should have been. His skin teemed with worms and lice that thrived on the festering sores that covered his body. As the apparition neared the screaming child, coughing wracked the withered figure, and it vomited phlegm and blood-flecked foam. Just as the man reached the child, he vanished.

The child quieted, but began screaming anew as another figure glided forward. Again, the apparition was ugly beyond belief, this time a woman whose dried skin was wrinkled like a prune and who walked with painful jerks with the help of two canes, one leg dragging helplessly behind. Her every movement told of aching joints, her muscles so weak with age that after every step, she paused to summon strength enough to take the next. Her face seemed shrunken, her glazed, blind eyes threatened to pop from their sockets, and her mouth caved inward over toothless gums. The claws of her hands gripped feebly at her canes as she tottered toward the child.

The woman faded from view as she neared the child, but the lad's wailing continued as the third figure started forward. It was the body of a man, dead, lying on a blanket. The vision floated toward the child, who screamed even louder than before. The dead man's face was contorted with pain, and his limbs were mutilated as if torn by a lion and trampled by an elephant. On looking closer, the Maharajah could see that the wounds were caked with blood, seared by the sun, as if the man had baked for days under the open sky after some horrible accident. Ants swarmed the corpse, sucking at the wounds and pulling at the scabs. The man had died a dirty, slow, tortured death.

On nearing the screaming child, this apparition faded and vanished, just as had the previous two. The Maharajah glanced at the far corner, looking for the fourth figure, but the last apparition had disappeared. No. Looking more closely, he could see it in the middle of the hall gliding soundlessly toward the child. The Maharajah could not make the figure out. It was vague and indistinct, shrouded in a red mist, yet the child seemingly had no trouble seeing it. He was not frightened now. He had stopped his crying and reached out gleefully toward the silent phantom. A smile spread across the child's face, all the terror evoked by the previous spirits gone. He gurgled happily as the figure approached, as it reached out and offered a morsel of honey cake. In no time the infant had downed the sweet and was sucking greedily at his fingers, a look of contentment spread over his face. As the father watched, the child's eyelids fluttered in sleepy satisfaction, the little head nodded drowsily, and the babe was suddenly in a deep slumber. His breathing became deep and rhythmic, slow, slower, even slower, and then, before the horrified father, his son's breathing stopped. Sprinting from his chair, the Maharajah raced to the corner where the boy lay.

"Poisoned!" he screamed. "He's been murdered!"

Behind him, the Devil burst into wild laughter; and at that moment, as the Maharajah stumbled toward the dead child, his son vanished. Enraged, the monarch turned toward his guest.

"You have killed my son!" he shouted. "You have broken the bargain!"

"Me? Killed your son? Whatever do you mean?" As the Maharajah stood, bewildered, Satan wiped tears of laughter from his eyes. "You must be imagining things."

"Bring my son!" the Maharajah ordered one of his servants, and then to Satan, added, "We shall see if I am imagining things."

In no time the servant returned, carrying the Maharajah's son, who, though crying from having been wakened, was certainly healthy and alive. At the sight of the lad, the Maharajah sighed joyously and clasped the child to him, as if to convince himself the lad was real and safe and that the scene he had just witnessed had been, indeed, a vision. Assured finally, the monarch sent the babe back to its crib and turned, only to see the cards on the table. A shiver ran through him. His son was not safe after all!

Satan grinned wickedly. His white teeth were more pointed than ever, his chin sharper, his ears more angular, and behind his eyes, the fire danced brighter than before.

"Won't you deal?" he asked, indicating the empty chair across from him.

In a daze, the Maharajah sat down. The cards lay before him, but he could not will his hands to pick them up. It was as if someone wanted him to reach into a slithering mass of cobras and stir them into a frenzy. He was afraid! Fear swept through him, crushing his innards, suffocating him. Choking, he fought the fear back so that he could breathe, and finally, gingerly, reached out for the cards. To lose would be to kill his son. Therefore, he must win.

He pushed the cards across the table to Satan.

"Do you want me to cut?" the Devil asked mockingly. "Aren't you afraid to let me touch the cards? Aren't you afraid I'll cheat?" The Maharajah did not answer, but silently retrieved the pack after it had been cut. Forcing his fingers to obey, he dealt two hands. Sweat dampened his palms, and a trickle of perspiration stung one eye. When the two hands were dealt, Satan casually fanned open his five cards and smiled. The Maharajah did not dare to touch his own cards, but slowly he opened them. Two pairs!

There were two pairs! For a moment, joy welled in him, but instantly he suppressed his happiness. Perhaps two pairs would not be good enough. Nines and fives were not, after all, two very good pairs. Satan could have better. Thus, the Maharajah checked his joy, though he could not entirely extinguish the flame of hope within him.

"One," Satan demanded, discarding a card.

The Maharajah's heart sank as he dealt the single card. Satan too might have two pairs and was hoping for a full house. And if he had two pairs, one of them must be higher than nines. Rather than draw one card, as he had decided, the Maharajah reconsidered. Carefully, he weighed the odds, stared hard at his two pairs, as if he could elicit from them the solution to his problem. If the devil did have two pairs, then the Maharajah needed only three of a kind to win. That being so, he should discard all but the two nines. Reluctantly, he kept just the nines and drew three new cards.

For a long time, the Maharajah did not look to see what he had drawn, but simply held the cards in his trembling fingers. He could feel Satan's mocking gaze from across the table. The Devil seemed pleased with his hand. Finally, cautiously, the Maharajah peeked at the cards he had drawn. The first, a jack. No good. The next card, a seven, also no good. The Maharajah's hopes sank. But then the last card. A nine. That made three of a kind! If Satan had not filled his full house but had just two pairs, the Maharajah would win!

"Three of a kind," he said abruptly. "Did you fill your house?" Shaking, fear mixed with hope, he dashed his cards on the table, revealing the three nines.

"I did not fill a full house," Satan said. He paused. The Maharajah waited. "But then, I was not hoping for a full house. I had these"—he revealed four spades—"and drew this." He did not reveal the last card, but held it tauntingly so the Maharajah could not see it. If it were a spade, the monarch's three nines would lose to the flush. If it were not a spade, the Maharajah would win. Finally, smiling, Satan turned the card face up. The queen of spades.

"No!" the Maharajah screamed. "It cannot be!" As if struck by lightning, he collapsed, mumbling, in his chair. "No … no … It cannot be. My son … My only son …"

Across the table, Satan rocked with laughter. "Did I not tell you that I do not lose? Did you really believe you had a chance? Did you really think you could defeat *Satan*?" And for a long time, he laughed, with tears of merriment rolling down his cheeks.

When the Devil's amusement finally subsided, the Maharajah rose shakily from his chair. "If you will excuse me …" he mumbled.

"I will depart," Satan assured him, his eyes twinkling wickedly, "now that my business is completed. Your son and I will meet four times in the future. I do *so* want him to make a wise decision." With the diabolical fires dancing behind his eyes, Satan murmured, "To live … or not to live."

Abruptly, he gestured adieu and vanished, leaving a red mist where he had just stood.

It was many weeks after Satan's visit that the Maharajah emerged from his chambers, where he had cloistered himself with nothing but his grief. During the first of those weeks, he had mourned over his defeat to the Devil. Later, he began to consider how he might yet thwart Satan's plans. The Devil had promised to appear four times to his son. He had also mentioned that men turned bitter on being made aware of sickness, old age, and death.

Three horrific visions had appeared prior to the card game, depicting sickness, old age, and death. The fourth vision he had not been able to make out. All this convinced the Maharajah that Satan would appear to his son as a sick man, an old man, and a dead man. What the fourth appearance would be, the Maharajah could not guess. These appearances, he assumed, would convince his son that life was not worth living. Satan would drive the boy to commit suicide.

That much the Maharajah had deduced. Putting his grief behind him, he resolved to thwart Satan's plans. He would keep his son ignorant of sickness, old age, and death. Thus, the Maharajah banished from the court anyone who was elderly or infirm, and commanded that whenever the boy left the palace, a party of horsemen was to ride ahead in order to clear the road of any sick or old men or women. Furthermore, the monarch instructed the boy's tutor to avoid mentioning these aspects of life to the lad. In brief, the boy was to be raised with no knowledge at all of sickness, old age, or death. In this way, the Maharajah tried to assure himself, his son would become stable, optimistic, and happy; and thus he would thwart Satan's plan to drive his son to commit suicide.

So it was that the young prince came to be raised amongst the young and healthy children of the kingdom by servants who were clear-eyed and handsome. The Maharajah's decision seemed to be a good one, for the prince's laughter could always be heard ringing through the castle, and the tunes he whistled and hummed always lilted jauntily in the sunny corners of the palace. He was a gay, smooth-limbed boy, and his tutor found him eager to learn and easy to teach, for the child had a swift, agile mind.

The Maharajah was delighted with his son and came to love him more as the child grew from a toddler who played in the nursery to a lad who loved to ride his father's horses through the rice fields and hills. The boy enjoyed the outdoors; read avidly; spent hours carving figurcs from ebony, ivory, and jade; and played the lute with an abandon that drove listeners to tap their toes and want to dance. As the boy matured, he developed a skill and style in both his carving and his music that was astonishing in a lad. His carvings became exceptional works of art and his music worthy of the greatest musicians. Best of all, the boy grew to love the Maharajah's people. Soon he came to establish schools in the villages and to devote hours teaching reading and writing, music and art to the youngest of the Maharajah's subjects. He developed the custom when walking amongst the villagers to bring food to those most in need. Yes, the Maharajah was pleased to have a son so gifted and creative, so well attuned to nature, to his people and to his environment, and so loving and well-loved. And yes, the boy was fond of his father, adored his beautiful mother, and openly admired his tutor, whose side he rarely left. A more perfect son the Maharajah could not have wished for. And yet, as the child grew into maturity, the Maharajah became apprehensive. He could not believe that so happy a young man, his son, would stoop to take his own life! But Satan … There was Satan to reckon with.

While the Maharajah worried, life went on normally in the palace. At fourteen, his son had become a horseman unequalled in the region; at fifteen, his carvings were said to be the best in all the East and his music as good as any in all of India. And, as he matured further, he devoted more and more of his time to teaching the village young and assisting the impoverished. He delighted in life and loved his parents and his tutor. That such a one would take his own life was not possible. And thus, the Maharajah lulled himself into believing that Satan's plans had been thwarted—until the day his son turned seventeen.

On that day, the prince went riding with his tutor and some close friends, as they were wont to do; and as always, a party of horsemen preceded the prince to clear the way of any persons infirm or elderly. But at some point during the ride, whether due to an oversight on the horsemen's part or a change in route by the prince, the lad and his friends came across a leper lying by the side of the road.

The man was all but dead and a most hideous sight, for his skin rotted and stank, and his face was unrecognizable as such, with eye sockets gaping empty and open sores obliterating his other features. As they neared the man, he moaned, begging for water to quench his thirst and pleading for death to end his pain. The group halted and ministered to the man, but other than offering him water, there was little they could do.

The prince, of course, asked his tutor about the state of the man—for the prince had never seen sickness—and was shocked with grief to learn that the pain and anguish of disease was a common phenomenon in his father's kingdom.

"But why didn't you ever mention disease in my lessons?" the boy cried indignantly. "Certainly you have failed to educate me well if you have omitted discussion of such a normal occurrence."

The tutor, of course, could only shrug and answer noncommittedly.

The sight of the leper made a deep impression on the prince, and though he rarely spoke of the incident, his father noticed that the boy's life changed that day. His close relation to his tutor became less trusting, no doubt because the boy felt the tutor had betrayed or duped him; and the boy would often return from rides through the fields with his face full of sorrow and sit for hours brooding. This was unlike the happy prince of years past, and on questioning one of the lad's friends, the Maharajah would learn that the boy had seen a crippled bird or infected cow in the fields that day, and that the sight had moved him to tears.

One year after seeing the leper, on the day of his eighteenth birthday, the lad returned from an outing more agitated than usual. The tutor explained the prince's agitation to the Maharajah: along the highway they had met a woman gnarled and weary with age. Her face had been wrinkled like a hideous monkey, her gums toothless, her skin veined blue and thin as parchment. She had been leaning on two canes, too old to dodder more than one or two steps, too blind to make out where she was going, and too deaf to hear the prince's party as they addressed her. The prince, the tutor continued, had asked what matter of being she was and had been horrified when the tutor explained old age.

"You mean this is a natural state?" the prince had asked, aghast. "All creatures someday become as hideous as this hag?"

The tutor had nodded sadly, and for the remainder of the ride home the prince spoke to no one. That night, the boy could not sleep. The vision of the hag smoldered in him. He alternately tossed and turned in bed and paced the floor in the darkness. The thought that all people became as decrepit as that hag was unbearable. It affected him more than the vision of the leper a year before. Disease and sickness were perhaps common, he thought, but they were not inevitable. Old age—if the prince could believe his tutor, and of that he was no longer certain—was a certainty.

For the next weeks and months, the young prince could not forget the old hag. Everywhere he went, he was reminded of her; everything he saw called her to mind. Whereas until now he had found the world beautiful, desirable, alive, now he could only see that every aspect of it was doomed to old age and decay. The rice in the fields was withering, the grapes in the vineyard rotted on the vine, the Maharani's beauty was no longer radiant, his favorite stallion was too old to be ridden, the birds winging southward spelled the last days of the summer. And so it went. Whereas before the prince had seen only the beauty and the mystery of life, now he could see only sorrow and decay.

The Maharajah watched anxiously as his son became moody and introspective. He urged the lad to go into the fields as he was wont to do, but his son declined, saying he abhorred nature, it was so ugly. When urged to return to his hours in the villages to teach the young and help the poor, he shrugged with indifference. The Maharajah continued to provide his son with ebony, ivory, and jade for his sculpting, and the prince would forget his sorrow in his art. But soon the exquisite, remarkable figures he created portrayed nothing but gnarled, misshapen old men and women, until one day the prince threw one of his most exquisite pieces onto the tiled floor in a rage, shattering it into hundreds of shards. He would carve no more, he declared. He turned to his lute for pleasure, but soon the tunes turned slow and sad, descended into dirges, until one day he smashed the instrument in anger and vowed he would never play again. Life disgusted him.

The Maharajah now became seriously concerned over his son's wretchedness. Whatever doubts he had had regarding the leper and the old hag—whether or not they were chance sightings or Satan appearing in disguise—were now dispelled. This wretchedness that his son was enduring was the Devil's work. And Satan's threat seemed almost to be fulfilled. It did not take much imagination, thought the Maharajah, to conceive of the prince taking his own life now. Especially if Satan were to appear to him once or twice more!

On the morning of the prince's nineteenth birthday, the palace was gay with laughter, and the prince took one of his now infrequent rides to escape the cheerful atmosphere, which he found repugnant. While riding alone through the hills, whose worn rocks and folded slopes reminded him of the old age to which he would inevitably fall victim, he noticed birds circling a patch of shrubs. He rode near to investigate.

When he reached the bushes, a gruesome sight lay before the prince. It was the body of a man, mangled and trampled, burned by the sun, pecked and torn by the birds, crawling with ants. Though the prince had never seen or heard of death, he realized instantly that this was the inevitable conclusion to life.

After gaping at the horrible corpse for a few moments, the young prince turned his horse and fled. Gallop as he might, he could not escape the vision he had witnessed. Only months before life had seemed so glorious to him! But now, he knew, it was a mockery. Disease and decay and death lurked behind every transient beauty. That flower over there, bright in a corner between the rocks, would soon wither and perish. That tree, fertile and green now, was only the forerunner of gaunt limbs raised beseechingly toward the sky. How could he ever, he wondered, have loved such gossamer images? How could he ever again behold an object without being aware of its future repulsiveness? How could he continue to live in such a world of horrors?

On returning to the palace, the prince withdrew to his chambers. He attempted to eschew his thoughts by shaping a bit of ivory with a knife, but as before, he smashed the carved figure against the wall when he found his fingers had formed a replica of the dead man he had just seen. His art disgusted him, just as his surroundings did. Everything reminded him of death, decay, and disease. When his father came into the room to console him, the boy did not look up. Why should he? Why should he be polite? Loving? His father would soon be dead—and his death would be all the more difficult to bear if the prince loved him too much.

The monarch was instantly aware of the anguish in his son's eyes, and he knew without having to be told that Satan had appeared for the third time to the boy. The Maharajah was distressed that the prince would not even bother to acknowledge his presence, and he instantly resolved that action must be taken in order to prevent the boy from taking his own life. All night, the Maharajah fretted and pondered. The next morning, he ordered that knives, swords, daggers, indeed any and all sharp objects, be removed from the castle. Also, any rope strong enough to serve as a hangman's noose. It was clear to the Maharajah that his son balanced on the edge of committing suicide. Satan had appeared three times; he had promised four visits. The Maharajah had no doubt the next visit would come soon, and that it would be designed to push his son over the edge. By removing all means by which one could commit suicide, he hoped he might save his son's life.

The Maharajah also decided to seek advice, but he did not know where to turn. He spoke first to the Maharina, but though she shared his fears, she was at a loss to help. Both of them concluded something had to be done, and it had to be done before Satan's next visit. Together they decided the Maharajah should visit the temple in town; perhaps the elders there might be of assistance.

The Maharajah explained his predicament to the three wisest of the temple elders. Options and various approaches were discussed, but after endless hours the four of them were no nearer a solution than at the start. At wits' end, one of the elders suggested they seek advice from a wandering mendicant who had arrived a few days earlier. This monk was apparently regarded far and wide for his wisdom, both his innate wisdom and the wisdom imparted him by the countless persons he had met over his many years. His skin was dried from the sun, and the whole of his body was shriveled from lack of nourishment. He was bereft of possessions but for his dingy robe, apparently once red but now faded and dirty, the color of the dust of the road he trod.

Despite his appearance, the Maharajah approached him. It took but a few minutes for the Maharajah to conclude this was a truly religious man, a man committed to his gods, a man steeped in wisdom and experience. Might this man, the Maharajah asked himself, possess—perhaps—knowledge of how one might foil the devil? He spoke with the bhakti about little things, where he had traveled, whom he had met, why he wore a red robe rather than the more usual yellow of the mendicants; and then moved to more significant issues, probing his views on nature, life, love, and the world in general. He found, as he had hoped, the bhakti to be a man of education, well-learned and thoughtful. So, he explained the poker game with Satan and explained the matter of his son.

"Bring me to the boy," the mendicant said after his host had told him all that had befallen his son. "Bring me to the boy and I will do what I can." The two of them decided the monk would come to the palace the next day.

Upon the arrival of the monk, the Maharaja cautiously sent for his son. This calm ascetic, placid in his robe, so removed and aloof from the world—could he persuade the young prince that suicide would be a poor decision? The Maharajah hoped against hope as he waited for his son to meet the bhakti.

The prince entered the room with eyes downcast, his expression disconsolate. There was no glimmer of interest as his father introduced the bhakti. The son hardly looked up, paid no heed to the man. Nor did the bhakti speak. A deep silence gripped the three of them. When the silence had become almost unbearable, the bhakti spoke softly, almost in a whisper.

"You have endured much suffering." The monk did not pose the phrase as a question, but rather as a statement, a quiet statement of fact. The boy made no response, but a slight flutter of his eyelids evidenced agreement with the mendicant's judgment. After a long silence, the monk continued. "Even though you are young in years, you are old in the ways of the world. Already you know one of the Four Noble Truths: the Noble Truth of Suffering. It is this: birth is suffering."

The boy looked up. The ascetic seemed to have struck a chord. Again, a slight flutter of the boy's eyelids. The monk continued.

"Yes, birth is suffering, illness is suffering, decay is suffering, death is suffering. Separation from those we love is suffering. The very essence of life is suffering. That …" The bhakti paused. "That is the First Noble Truth: the Noble Truth of Suffering.

"And this is the Second Noble Truth: the Noble Truth of the Cause of Suffering. The cause of suffering is thirst. Thirst for living that leads to rebirth and continued suffering."

As the bhakti spoke in slow, measured tones, the prince warmed to his words. This devoted emissary understood him. They understood each other. Birth was suffering; that made sense. Birth was the cause of life, and life, as the prince knew, was a hideous torture, a slow, inexorable decay, a rotting that led to death. If one thirsted for this life, the prince knew, death was not a final escape from the torture. Absolute death—parinirvana—could only be reached by the pure. Thirsting for life caused one to be impure, caused karma to collect on the soul; and if one were impure, death was not the portal to parinirvana, but the gateway to rebirth. Hence, the prince agreed with the bhakti: birth was suffering and thirst was the cause of suffering. The prince listened carefully as the bhakti continued in a soporific monotone.

"This, oh, prince, is the Third Noble Truth: the Noble Truth of the Cessation of Suffering. Suffering ceases with the cessation of all thirst. Suffering ceases with the abandonment of passion, with the destruction of desire, with the death of love."

The Maharajah watched the effect of the bhakti's words on his son, for surely their effect was great. Whereas before the boy's expression had been of one sucking a particularly bitter lemon, now he wore the satisfied look of a child nibbling a honey cake. Would the monk nudge the boy to a place where he would no longer think of committing suicide?

"And this, oh, prince," intoned the bhakti, "is the Fourth Noble Truth: the Noble Truth of the Path that leads to the cessation of suffering. Suffering ceases upon reaching complete detachment from all the concerns of secular existence. Such detachment is three-fold. First, one must suspend the will to accomplish, one must desire neither to mold nor to create. Second, one must move in blindness through the world, oblivious to one's surroundings. And third, one must abandon all concerns for people, both for others and one's self. This is the Noble Truth of the Path. For those who tread the Path, oh, prince, all suffering ceases."

To the delight of the Maharajah, his son seemed to crawl, however slowly, from the world of his despair to the vision presented by the mendicant. For the first time in many weeks, the prince spoke. "And how, bhakti," the prince asked, "does one tread the Path? How does one suspend one's will to accomplish? How does one move blindly through the world? How does one destroy one's concern for others and one's self? Enlighten me, please. What must I do?"

Something was stirring inside the boy, the Maharajah thought. For the first time in many months, it was as if a candle had been lit. His son's sorrows seemed to be melting. Perhaps the bhakti possessed a secret power over the prince. He seemed to draw the boy to him, to hypnotize him. Just see how the boy's face, so recently full of hate, now wore the expression of contentment. Was the transformation real?

"The path to detachment, to cessation of suffering,"

intoned the bhakti, "is the path I follow. When I stand, my hands hang beside me; when I sit, they lie folded in repose. For always they are content with passivity, wanting neither to shape this world nor build another. When I walk, I move through the world looking neither before me nor behind, glancing neither to the right of me nor to the left. When I withdraw into myself, I think not of where my mother dwells, nor of the house of my father. I do not recall the names of my brothers, nor of my sisters. Never does my mind concern itself with persons, neither with others nor myself."

The prince appeared entranced by the power of the bhakti. Was it being done? wondered the Maharajah. Was his son being saved from death?

"I move through the shadow of the world," the bhakti sang. "I know not where I slept last night, nor where I will lay down my head this evening. I know not what I eat nor who provides me with my food. I take no notice of other beings, neither learning their names nor seeing their faces. I close my eyes to my surroundings, oblivious alike to ugliness and beauty, pain and pleasure. I wander aimlessly through the impalpable universe. That, oh, prince, is how I tread the Path."

The bhakti rose slowly from his seat and beckoned to the Maharajah's son. He spoke in a whisper, yet it was as though he were calling to someone across a great chasm.

"To end thy suffering, oh, prince," he said, walking to the door, "come. Follow me. Throw off the fetters that chain you to life. Loose the ties that bind you to this world. Sever the bonds that knot thee to thine loved ones. Throw off thy earthly raiment and don the red robe of the mendicant. I go once more on my way. Join me!"

The bhakti paused at the door, and though he had only whispered, his voice, like thunder in the mountains, rolled and echoed on the walls and ceiling, calling, calling. The prince rose as if in a dream. He addressed his father, a faraway, somnolent look in his eye.

"My father, you have heard the bhakti's advice. You hear he urges me to follow him. You know how unhappy I've been these years past few years, you know how I now find only sorrow where once I found joy. To me it seems best to follow the counsel of the bhakti, to sever the ties that bind me to my life here with you and the Maharina. Joining the bhakti would, I think, lift the sadness from my soul. Do you agree if I leave and join the ways of the monk in his travels?"

The Maharajah sighed. In just a few minutes, the bhakti had seemingly worked a miracle. The sadness was gone from his son, as if the boy's soul had been quieted. He seemed to be at peace, his suffering behind him. The monarch nodded to the boy. He did not want to let his son go, but if he did not leave before Satan's promised fourth visit, he almost certainly would commit suicide.

"It is hard to let you leave the palace," the Maharajah said, "to let you leave the life you know here. But the choice, my son, is yours. You have free will, you are free to choose your destiny. Should you decide to leave …" He paused, gathering strength to say these last words, to give his blessing to his son's departure. "If you decide to leave, I bid you Godspeed."

Sorrowfully, the Maharajah turned to the bhakti. "I thank you from the depths of my heart. You have driven the sadness from my son's life. I don't know how to thank you."

"You must not thank me," the bhakti said. "Convincing men to follow in my footsteps is my calling."

"Perhaps," replied the Maharajah. "And yet I thank you."

"But you must not thank me," the bhakti repeated. "I do for your son what I would do for any man."

The monarch watched as the prince and the bhakti turned and strode out of the palace. The boy had neither kissed his father nor turned to wave adieu to his mother: he had already begun the process of detaching himself from this world. It was hard, the Maharajah thought, to watch his son walk away when he knew they would never meet again. Hard when he would never see his son's eyes light with pleasure at his mother's smile. Hard when he would never hear him play the lute for children dancing, radiant with joy. Hard to know his son had abandoned his carvings, would never again stroll in the villages of the kingdom and instruct the little ones and feed the poor who loved him so, would nevermore have the pleasure of riding his stallion across the plains and into the mountains to bathe in nature's splendor. Would never again walk into the palace with love alight on his face, striding to the Maharajah for a fond father-and-son embrace. And yet, he thought, how much harder it would have been if Satan had succeeded in his plans! If the boy had committed suicide! If he had quit this life!

The bhakti and the prince were now no more than a dot on the distant road, a minuscule swirl of red dust. The Maharajah continued to watch long after even the pinpoint of red had disappeared. He was sad at his son's departure but consoled himself that the bhakti had saved his son's life. Despite his desolation, the Maharajah let slip a wry smile at the thought he had cheated Satan. When Satan arrived for his fourth visit, he might well boast at the small victory of winning a hand of poker. But the true victory had been won by the Maharajah. His son lived!

ACKNOWLEDGMENTS

To acknowledge everyone who influenced this book would not be possible, so I will name but a few:

My wife Francine, who brews my coffee every morning, getting me in the mood to sit at the computer; my bother Jan, the artist, who commented on early versions of my works and urged me to continue when I first began writing (now some sixty years ago!); my editor Elizabeth Barrett, who has had the patience to review draft upon draft of these stories; Deborah Bailey of Barnstormer Design, who manages my website; Tom Holbrook of Piscataqua Press for crafting and publishing this book; my daughter France and my friends Pat Wine and Jerry Baker, who promote my books. And then the many others who have influenced me. The authors whose books I read, the teachers who corrected my essays when I was a student in the 1950s … Should I include the medical staff who pulled me through an illness two years ago when it was touch and go? Thank you all!

www.ingramcontent.com/pod-product-compliance
Lightning Source LLC
Chambersburg PA
CBHW020551310726
48979CB00008B/1170/J

* 9 7 8 1 9 5 0 3 8 1 4 0 1 *